Girl on Honeysuckle Avenue

Clark Graham

http://clarkgrahamauthor.com/

http:/facebook.com/elvenshore

elvenshore@gmail.com

See Sample Chapter of

Bullets and Blondes

At the end of this book

Contents

Chapter One

Austin set down his lunch tray. Looking out the window, he wished he was anywhere else instead of the school cafeteria. Only half over, the day had dragged on and on. The spring that beckoned him lay just a mere thin sheet of glass away.

"Hey, give me your lunch money." Koot, Derick, and Garth took the chairs around him. Koot and his gang everyone called them, the bullies the school knew about but wouldn't do anything about until one of them actually hurt another student. They weren't after lunch; they wanted drug money and didn't care how they got it.

"Money, what's that? I'm so rich I'm on the free student lunch program."

"Don't get smart with me or I'll meet you right outside school property and…"

"I wouldn't advise it." The three looked up to see Ricardo standing there. "Scram before I lose my temper."

Koot and his gang hurried and left.

"Thanks, Ricardo."

Ricardo sat down; his plate heaped with food. "Sure, anytime, Gilbert. I don't like those guys, always picking on people."

"Please don't call me that. People will hear you calling me that and then they'll start calling me that too."

"Sorry, *Austin*. You were Gilbert when I first met you in grade school, though. Old habits die hard."

"That was my mom registering me in school by my middle name. I don't know why it was so important to her at the time." Austin thought for a minute. "I wonder what people do who actually have lunch money?"

"Hide it in their shoe. Nowadays you can have your mom go to the school's website and buy a month of lunches at a time so you don't have to send them to school with lunch money for Koot to steal."

"I wish I could stand up to him."

"You need to put more meat on those bones first. I stood up to him in eighth grade. His buddies fled at the first sight of blood."

"What happened?"

"Let's just say, his front two teeth aren't standard equipment. He don't mess with me anymore."

"I wish I could have been there."

"You did miss a lot of school back in the day. I'm glad you're healthy now. Say, do you want to go with me to the weight room? Coach is unlocking it right after school these days."

"Scrawny old me?"

Ricardo grabbed one of his three burgers and put it on Austin's tray. "You can't get big eating those salads. Here, wolf that down."

Austin looked at the greasy burger. "I can't eat all this."

"Fine, skip the salad."

Sighing, Austin took a bite out of the burger.

In each of his afternoon classes, he saw the girls looking down at him. At least he felt like they were. One smiled at him, but the rest went out of their way to avoid him. How did he get to be a senior in high school without having had a single girlfriend the whole time? Ricardo had women falling all over him. Of course, he did; he played football. A varsity lineman for all four years.

As he took notes in class, he wrapped himself in his own world and ignored everyone else. The burger, he couldn't ignore. It sat there swishing around every time he moved. *Why did I let him talk me into that?* He already knew the answer. He needed Ricardo. Without Ricardo as a friend, he would be an easy target to everyone who ever wanted to feel like a man by pushing around the skinny guy. Ricardo had been a good friend from grade school on up. The big guy had a heart of gold.

He met at the gym where twenty football types stood in line waiting for the coach. He was as tall as most of them, but a lot skinnier. Ricardo dwarfed them all. Whistling, the coach walked in, unlocked the door, and greeted each boy as they passed. "Well, hello, Austin, I'm happy to see you here."

Austin's mouth gaped open. He didn't have an idea how the coach knew his name. If he would have read it off a roster it would have been *Gilbert*, because of how his mother had registered him. "Hi, Coach."

Austin changed into his PE clothes and sat at the first empty weight machine. He pulled down with all his might, but the bar would not move. He tried again, with the same result. Scanning the room, he saw the football types pushing up and pulling down on their bars over and over again. *Wow.* He glanced over at the exit trying to figure out how to escape without anyone seeing him.

"Here, let me help." The coach stood over him. Pulling the pin out of the heavier weight, he put it up to a lighter weight. "Try that, see how it feels."

Austin pumped it up and down a few times. "That's great."

"Yeah, Ricardo was the last to use this machine. Nobody in here except him could move that much weight. I'm sure gonna miss him on the team next year. I'll go to his games. Just have to wait and see which scholarship he accepts."

"He has a scholarship?"

"Yep, five of them. I thought he would have told you."

"He didn't. He probably didn't want to hurt my feelings. I might not be able to go to college." Austin stood up and walked over to Ricardo. "Why didn't you tell me you had scholarships?"

Ricardo gently let go of the weights he had been pushing. "I haven't decided if I'm going yet."

Austin put his hands on his hips. "Yes, you're going, or I'm going to beat you."

Ricardo leaned against the wall, he laughed so hard. He wiped his eyes when he caught his breath. "I guess I'll have to go then. I don't want to get beaten."

After the workout, Austin put his PE clothes in his locker and started to get dressed.

"Dude, what are you doing?" A stark-naked Ricardo asked him. He had a towel over his shoulder but he made no effort to cover up and no one would blame him. "You have to take a shower. You stink."

"I'm so embarrassed."

"No one's looking. Come on."

Putting his street clothes back in his locker, Austin wrapped a towel around himself and followed Ricardo into the shower. He figured if anyone were looking, it would be Ricardo they'd be looking at.

After getting dressed, the two of them walked home together. Ricardo only had to walk the five blocks down Ramsey. Austin would have to walk another six blocks to get to his home. He didn't need to call to let his mom know he stayed after school because he thought he'd still arrive about the same time the bus would.

"Why do you suppose big guys like me, who aren't all that good at scholastics, get scholarships, and guys like you who are good at scholastics, don't?"

"I don't know how good I am, but I almost got a scholarship. I've applied for several more and with my mother's income being so low, they assure me I'll be eligible for a lot of financial aid."

"I wish you luck." Ricardo stopped at his house. "See you."

Chapter Two

Austin crossed Ramsey Street to Honeysuckle Avenue. He walked behind several houses. He walked on that side of the street because the wide spot in the road made it easier going than on the grass. The chain-link fences next to him had slats in them to improve the privacy to the back yards of the houses he walked next to. It didn't work well though. He could both see over and through the fences.

Right as he made ready to cross the street, he spied a blonde girl in a backyard. She looked like a movie star laying there in a white bikini soaking up the sun. He didn't realize he was staring until she noticed him and let out a yelp. She stood up and ran towards the house, but then stopped suddenly and turned. At first, she folded her arms and scowled, but then her face softened and she smiled and waved.

Awkwardly, he waved back.

"What are you looking at, kid?" A frowning man had come out on the back porch.

"Um, bikini, no, er, girl. Um, her." He pointed.

"Move along."

The girl had a case of giggles by this point. Flushed red, Austin turned and crossed the street.

The single-wide trailer lay halfway down the road, the only place his mother's income could afford to rent. Austin hated it. The landlord promised to fix things right away, but months would go by before he got around to it.

When he entered, his mother coughed as she said, "You're late. I was beginning to worry about you."

"Sorry I'm late. It's because I don't have a cell phone as to why I didn't call."

"Don't get smart with me. You know I can't afford another cell phone. I can barely pay for the one I've got." Sitting down at the kitchen table she picked up her inhaler and breathed in deeply.

"You're bad today?"

Catching her breath, she put it back down. "I'm worried about you. You missed the bus again. Where were you?"

Austin grimaced. She didn't used to use the inhaler much, but now it was almost constant. "I stayed after to lift weights."

Her eyes narrowed. "Now I know you're lying. Are you into drugs?"

"No, Mom. How can I afford drugs? Ricardo thinks I'm too scrawny so he talked me into going to the weight room after school."

"Oh." She leaned back against the wall.

Austin hated the fact that all he had to do was say Ricardo in the sentence and his mom would believe anything he said afterward. As a kid, he tested the theory by saying "Ricardo and I are going to outer space."

Not only did his mother believe him, but she expressed her concerns to Ricardo's mother, who didn't have a clue what his mom was talking about.

"Are you feeling okay, Mom?"

"I'll be all right. Tell me about your day."

"It's the same every day, Mom. Go to school, go to class, eat lunch, come home."

"Did you meet anyone new?"

He could still see the image of the girl in the white bikini smiling and waving at him. "No. No one new at school."

"I'm sorry to disappoint you, son, but I have a pizza coming. I don't have the energy to cook tonight. I know you think I spend too much money on takeout food, but I just can't."

"It's okay, Mom." He pulled out his books and spread them out on the table. Sitting across from her, he worked on his homework. He glanced at her as she rested her back against the wall. Her ashen-colored face worried him. Finally, he said, "Do you think you should see a doctor?"

She glared at him. "No, never again. I can't even afford the co-pays. No more talk of doctors. I'll be just fine." Leaning back against the wall, she closed her eyes.

He sighed and went back to his homework. When the doorbell rang, she stood up and answered it. Austin quickly tucked his books and papers into his backpack. When his mother put the pizza on the table, she took another breath into the inhaler before sitting down.

"Eat up," she smiled.

After his third piece, he reached for his fourth. His mother had half-finished her first. He pulled his hand back. Her eyes closed and she leaned back against the wall again. "Aren't you going to finish?"

"I'm good." She didn't open her eyes.

"I'll save the rest of it for breakfast. It's my favorite breakfast food, you know."

"What's that, dear?"

"Cold pizza." He shook his head. He knew she wasn't listening again.

"That's nice, dear."

After he finished his homework, he read the book he had checked out from the schools' library. He came back into the kitchen. His mother had slipped off to bed. He picked up a book and read for a while. The girl on Honeysuckle Avenue still clung to his memory. She stood there, in his mind, smiling and waving. No girl had ever smiled at him like that. He had to meet her. *What are the chances that she'll ever be in the backyard sunbathing again?* He sighed. Putting down his book, he headed off to bed. He knew his dreams would be nice this night.

Chapter Three

As the morning bus drove by the house, Austin tried to peek in the windows. He felt guilty, telling himself he was a peeping Tom at heart, but he wanted another glance at the girl. The lights were off, so he leaned back in his seat for the ride to school. '

The first three periods were long. He had a hard time concentrating. He kept thinking about the beautiful girl who waved at him.

After getting some food, he sat down next to Ricardo. "Do you know the girl on Honeysuckle Avenue? Well, not on Honeysuckle, but her backyard faces it. She's blonde. She has to live on the side street there so the back of her house is on Honeysuckle."

"Wow." Ricardo eyed him up and down. "You're talking about a girl. You never do that. Are you feeling okay?"

Austin huffed. "Yes, I'm fine. I'm talking about a girl. Not a mere girl, but a goddess. Blonde hair, blue eyes. She smiled at me. You must know her. You've asked out every girl of the senior class. She looks to be our age."

"Hmm. A goddess, huh? I'll have to meet this girl."

"No, you don't. I saw her first."

"That's not the way it works, my friend." Ricardo laughed. "No worries. I promise not to step on your toes. I only asked out every girl in the senior class. I wanted them to have at least one date before leaving high school. I figured the ones with boyfriends would tell me no. Well, some of them didn't. Boy, did that cause me some trouble. It's a good thing I'm big. I'm done with that. I've asked out every one of them. I know the houses you are talking about. She can't be going to school here. I would have known about her."

Austin's shoulders sagged. "I want to meet her. She seems nice."

Ricardo took a bite out of his burger. "Wait. I have heard about her. Bob tried to talk to her. Her old man came out on the front porch with a shotgun. You need to stay away from that one. She's trouble."

"Yes, he chased me away, too, but he didn't have a shotgun."

Ricardo stood up and yelled across the cafeteria. "Hey, Bob. Austin wants to know about that girl who lives across the street from you."

There was a whole lot of laughing all around. Austin sunk down in his chair, wishing he could disappear. Ricardo had no inhibition. You could either have Ricardo as a friend, or you could have secrets. You couldn't have both.

Bob set his tray down. "What do you want to know about her, Austin?"

He cleared his throat as he sat up. "What's her name? Why isn't she going to school? What all do you know about her? That's what I want to hear."

"Her name starts with an L. That's all I remember. The bushy-haired guy with a shotgun said, 'Get inside, L...' something. I was looking down both barrels at the time and backing up as fast as I could. She's cute, but definitely not worth dying over. I think she's homeschooled. The post office delivers packets to her from some online type of high school. I see them on her doorstep about once a week. That's all I know."

"Thanks." Austin scanned the room. At least half of the people were smiling as they watched Bob talk to him.

Bob and Ricardo talked about football the rest of lunch. Austin, stared out the window. He shouldn't have. Seeing another beautiful day out there that he wasn't enjoying just tormented him more. *I wonder if she's out there sunbathing while I sit here.* He had to shake the thought from his mind and go to class.

After school, Ricardo came up to him. "You coming to weight lifting today?"

"No, Mom's been sick. I have to go make sure she's all right."

"Hmm. Your mom's been sick all the years I've known you. How is this any different?" Ricardo gave him a sideways glance. "It's the girl, isn't it?"

"Well," he shrugged. "It is Mom, but it's the girl too. I just want to see her again. I don't even have to talk to her."

"I see. Go ahead, Romeo. I can lift weights without you."

"I'll try and make it tomorrow. Really, I will."

"No, You won't. You're smitten." Ricardo walked away.

Smitten? Austin didn't like the sound of that. He mulled over the word during the bus ride home. Getting off at the stop before his so he could walk past the back of the house, he slowed way down when he reached the fence line. He peeked over at the house every other footstep. *No girl.* He sighed, then crossed the street.

Chapter Four

His mother's coughing woke Austin up. He tapped on her door. "Are you okay, Mom?"

She cleared her throat. "It's so nice of you to check on me. What a good son you are. Now go back to sleep. I'll be fine."

"Mom, I'm worried. The coughing and breathing are getting worse. Let's take you to the walk-in clinic at least. Let them check you out."

"We'll talk about it in the morning, dear."

Austin crawled back in bed. He knew what she meant. There would be no mention of it in the morning and if he tried to bring it up, she'd shut him down. He tossed and turned instead of sleeping. He alternately thought of the girl and worried about his mother.

He finally fell asleep with only an hour and a half to spare before the alarm went off. It jarred him awake. He jumped out of bed and shut it off. Straightening the bedsheets, he headed into the kitchen. To his surprise, his mother wasn't there. He went down the hall to check on her. Her door hung open. The cluttered room lay empty. He checked out the window for her car, but it was gone. *I hope she went to the walk-in clinic.*

He made and ate his breakfast. Heading into the shower, he saw the landlord's latest fix. Vise grip pliers grabbed onto the shower's faucet. The knob had fallen off so the landlord improvised. Austin turned the vice grips and water flowed from the showerhead. *At least this fix works.*

He dried off, dressed, then headed for the bus. If he missed it today, he'd be so late walking to school, he wouldn't see a reason to go. His mother wouldn't mind. She never minded him missing school. She had hated school growing up and never graduated. To him, school was a way out of poverty and he worked hard at it. His hope of getting a scholarship hadn't worked out yet, but he had several applications in.

As he stepped out the door, he wondered again, where she had gone. *Oh, well.* He walked over to the bus stop. As the bus drove past the girl's house, he spotted her in the backyard waving.

His heart raced as he waved back vigorously. *Wait, was she waving at me?* Scanning the bus, he didn't see anyone else waving back. Several of the other students *were* staring at him, so he shrunk down in the seat. *Was she waving at someone across the street?* His happy heart melted into a puddle of self-misery.

As he stepped off the bus, he headed towards his first class of the day. History was his favorite subject, but the monotone voice of the teacher didn't help things. He soon found himself nodding off.

"Austin, are you with us?" The teacher stood over his desk. "Class is over. You'd better hustle along to your next one."

Embarrassed, Austin stood in the back of the next class so he wouldn't have a repeat performance of history.

When lunch came around, he found Ricardo sitting next to him at the table. "I've never seen you fall asleep at lunch before."

"Rough night. Mom is really sick. She wasn't around when I woke up. I only hope she has visited a walk-in clinic."

"I'll call her." Ricardo pulled out his cell phone. "Miss M. How are you doing today? Okay. Austin was wondering where you were since you weren't there when he left for school. All right, I'll tell him." Putting his phone away, he said. "She felt good this morning so she went to get some groceries. She tried to get back before you left, but didn't make it. She's home now."

"Who goes shopping at six in the morning? She's never done that before. She's lying."

"One way to find out. See if there are some new groceries in the house."

"And what would I say to her? I can't call her a liar to her face."

"You have a point." Ricardo bit his burger, then put one on Austin's tray. "Weight lifting today?"

Austin took a bite. "Sure."

"How is it going with the beauty queen?"

"She waved as the bus passed. I don't know what she waved at. It could have been me. It could have been she likes busses. It could have been someone else, or the sunshine, I don't know, but she waved."

"Just pretend she waved at you. It'll make you feel better."

21

"I can do that. Do you think I'm just being silly?" Austin took another bite out of the burger.

Ricardo laughed. "Love makes silly fools out of all of us. It's normal."

Austin made it through the next three classes without falling asleep. Coach smiled as he entered the weight room. The rest of the room filled up quickly, including Ricardo. Austin found a machine in the middle. He had to read the plaque that told him how to use it. Moving the peg to a lot less weight, he began his workout. An hour later, after the shower, they headed home.

Ricardo talked about how badly he would miss being in high school, how much he loved being on the Timberwolves football team for the last four years. Austin mostly kept quiet. Deep in his thoughts about his mother and thinking about the mystery girl, he only half-listened.

"Well, what do you think?"

"Um, what do I think about what?"

Ricardo put his hands on his hips. "It's the girl, isn't it?"

"What do I think?"

"Should I go to Moscow, Pullman, or Seattle to school? I have offers from all three and several others, but I've ruled them out already."

"You won't like Seattle. Moscow and Pullman are only seven miles apart and you can come home on the weekends so your mom can do your laundry. Pullman has a better program. So, I'd go there."

"That's what I was thinking." His smile disappeared. "What about you. Any bites?"

"Not, yet. I'm filling out applications anyway. I'm trying to get into Moscow."

"Well, little buddy, say hello to your mother for me."

After saying goodbye, Austin turned the corner onto Honeysuckle. He slowed down as he neared the girl's house.

Chapter Five

"Well, hello there."

Austin stopped, looked up and down the street. "A talking tree?"

The tree giggled, "No, silly. It's me. Lisa. You know, the girl you ogled a couple of days ago."

"Ogled?" he tried to peek through the branches, but couldn't see anything. "I don't think I ogled you. I took a long hard look, but I don't think it rose to the level of ogle."

Another giggle came from the tree.

"Can you come down, so I can see you?" Austin asked.

"No. Heavens, no. He doesn't know I'm talking to you. As far as he knows, I'm just climbing a tree. If he sees me talking to you, he'll come out."

"Who's he?"

"I can't answer that question, and if you ask it again, I can't talk to you anymore. I've got to go. Stay there long enough for me to get into the house, then you can walk past."

"Wait, when can I talk to you again?"

"Same time tomorrow."

"Oh, okay." He waited until he heard the door slam before walking the rest of the way home. He slipped into the house quietly. His ear-to-ear smile would be a dead giveaway to his mother that something had happened. He wasn't ready to talk about her yet.

The smile quickly disappeared. His mother sat, asleep, at the table. A stack of mail sat in front of her. A letter from the University of Idaho was on top of the pile. Setting it aside, Austin thumbed through the rest of the stack. A brochure on the bottom read, Living with COPD. An emergency room follow-up was with it. He read through it. Sticking the pile back in front of his mother, he checked the fridge. There were no new groceries in there. Most of what was there needed to be tossed out.

He sat down across from her. Eyeing the envelope from U of I, he hesitated opening it. It could be good news, but it could be bad news also. His future depended on the contents. Holding his breath, he gently tore it open. The first line read: Congratulations, you have been admitted to the University of Idaho.

"Yes!"

His mother looked up. "Oh, hello Austin. Good news?"

"I've gotten into the U of I."

"Congratulations."

He sat down the envelope. "I'll have to check on financial aid, but I can work that out later."

She sucked her inhaler. "Good. What do you think, a road trip? I think old Betsy can make it that far."

"I can do all the financial aid stuff from a computer. I'll stop in at the library."

"Oh, okay."

"Let's talk about the other thing."

She sat up in her chair. "What other thing?"

He picked the brochure out of the stack of mail. "You have COPD?"

"Oh, that. It's only their best guess. They want me to go through all sorts of tests and get poked and prodded. I told them I wouldn't do it."

"And then how are they supposed to help you, if they don't know what you have?"

"I'm okay."

He stood up so he could tower over her. "No, you're not. You're going to leave me all alone in the world. What am I supposed to do without you?"

"Okay, okay," she used her inhaler. "I'll get the stupid tests. Just not this month." She pushed the rest of the mail towards him. "I have all these bills to pay this month. I can't afford their tests until next month."

He leaned over the table and hugged her. "Thank you. I love you and want you around for a long time."

"I love you, too." She patted his arm. "I'll be okay."

"If you're feeling up to it, later on, we need to go grocery shopping. Despite what you told Ricardo, we don't have any food." He stood up and took all the old leftovers out of the refrigerator and disposed of them.

"We'll wait until you're feeling up to it."

"I'm fine. Let's go now." She stumbled as she stood. Austin caught her. Helping her down the steps into her faded blue Chevy Malibu. Austin hated the thing. Baling wire held up the rusted front bumper. The back passenger door wouldn't open because of the huge dent in it, something his mother refused to talk about. In fact, none of the dents and dings on the car were up for discussion.

It took a few minutes to start the car. *I could have walked and been there by now.* The grocery store lay only half a block away. Still, it would be nice to have a way to get the groceries home without having to carry them. He was happy that it was in the other direction from Lisa's house. He didn't want to get spotted in the old, beat-up car.

She parked in the handicapped parking. It didn't matter that she didn't have a pass. When he had asked her about it in the past, her simple reply would be, "There are lots of spots for the real handicapped people. They won't mind if I use one for a minute or two."

"Mom, it isn't right." Austin complained. Now that her condition had worsened, he didn't say anything. If she ever received a ticket, it would be a matter of not paying it, like all the parking tickets she had ever gotten.

When she tried to climb out the door, he told her to give him the list and stay in the car. She nodded. Handing him the list, she also gave him the EBT card.

Austin didn't know how much money the card had on it, but he knew they hadn't been shopping in a while, so he deviated from the list by buying fresh vegetables and fruit, something they rarely had. He also bought the heat-and-eat type items that made up his mother's list. To his surprise, the card worked for everything. He pushed the basket out the front door. There, surrounding his mother's car were police cars and an ambulance.

Chapter Six

Setting down the groceries, Austin ran over to her car. A big police officer with jet black hair held him back. "You can't go in there, son. Please step back."

"That's my mother!"

"I'm sorry, but let the paramedics do their job."

His mother lay on the ground as they worked on her. The paddles came out. They shocked her, but when they checked her heartbeat, the EMT would shake his head, and then try again. After twenty minutes, they gave up and put her in the back of the ambulance.

"I have to go with her."

The cop shook his head. "She's gone, son. Let them take her. I'll drive you down later. No sense in going now."

Austin collapsed in a heap in front of the car.

Later, after officer Fruean had driven him to the hospital, they let him go in to see his mother. A doctor stood near the body. "How did she die?" Austin asked.

"It looks like respiratory problems, but we won't know for sure until the autopsy." The doctor cleared his throat." She came in last night. We tried to keep her for a few days so we could put her on a ventilator, but she checked out against medical advice. I don't know if we could have helped her even then. She waited too long to come and see us."

"I know. She's stubborn that way." Austin took a deep breath. He nodded while wiping tears. "Goodbye—" he choked up. "Goodbye, Mom." He walked back out into the lobby. Officer Fruean still stood there.

"You got a place to stay, kid?"

"I—" his eyes widened. "I don't know. I'm still at the trailer, I guess. Until the landlord kicks me out."

"Come on. I'll drive you home."

As they passed the store, Austin gasped. "I forgot the groceries."

"Not to worry, I snagged them for you. They're in the back."

"Thank you."

As the officer pulled up to the house, he commented, "You live here?"

"Yes."

"I'm going to need to come in and check the place out."

"Why?"

"Because you're a minor and the conditions you're in are terrible."

"I'll be eighteen in five months. Besides, I don't think they're all that bad."

"Open the door please."

As the officer walked in, Austin stopped him. "Step around that spot in the kitchen floor. You'll fall through it if you don't."

"Thanks." He walked through. "The kitchen doesn't look too bad." He peeked into the living room. The carpet had holes in it and the furniture had exposed springs. "This one's bad though."

"We never go in there. We stay in the kitchen or our bedrooms. We've asked the landlord to fix the floor, but he hasn't gotten to it yet."

Fruean walked down the hall. Austin's room had a single bed and boxes where he put his clothes. Nothing else. When the officer opened his mother's room, a rat scurried under a floor-to-ceiling stack of garbage.

"I'm never allowed in here."

"That's a good thing. I'm deeming this trailer unfit for a minor to live in. You have a nearby relative?"

"I think Mom's folks live on the east coast somewhere. I'm not sure they're still around, though."

"Now's your chance to phone a friend."

"I don't have a phone, but I have a friend who lives a few blocks away."

"Pack your clothes. If I can get the last name, I can look up the number. I'll call ahead."

"Fuimaono."

"Oh, I have them in my phone. They're cousins of mine. You must be that friend I heard Ricardo talking about."

Austin shrugged. "I guess."

Officer Fruean called them up. "Hi, Auntie. I have a…" He covered the phone and leaned over to Austin. "What's your name?"

"Austin."

"I have an Austin here that needs a place to sleep for a few days, maybe longer. Do you have room?"

"Yes, have Gilbert come over right away."

He covered the phone again. "She's calling you Gilbert."

"That's my middle name. I used it when I first started grade school. She still uses it sometimes. My first name is Austin."

"Got it." Uncovering the phone, he said, "Thanks, Auntie. I'll bring him over right away."

Throwing his blanket on top of his box of clothes, Austin picked it up. "I'm ready."

Officer Fruean furrowed his brow. "That's all you collected in seventeen years of existence?"

"I have the groceries too."

"Right," Fruean smiled as he shook his head. "How could I have forgotten about the groceries?"

As they arrived at Ricardo's house, they all came out and hugged the officer and Austin. "What's going on?" Ricardo's mom asked.

"Austin's mom passed away this afternoon. I need to find a place for him to stay until I can make more permanent arrangements with CPS."

"Oh, no. Susan is dead? You poor boy." She took Austin in her arms and led him into the house.

He breathed deep, trying not to lose it.

"Hey, bro, what's happening?" Ricardo said.

"Susan passed." Mrs. Fuimaono said.

"Your mom!"

Austin opened his mouth but no words came out.

"Take your sisters and get his bed from his trailer. Bring it over here. We'll set it up for him in your room."

"No problem." Ricardo replied. He and his sisters headed out the door.

Mrs. Fuimaono led him into the living room and sat him down on the couch. "Tell me all about it."

Austin began telling her about her cough and shortness of breath and ended in the parking lot of the grocery store.

"We have to get your car back. I'll send the kids after it tomorrow."

Chapter Seven

"I'm not going to school today," Austin said. The bedroom had very little floor space left with the two beds in it.

"Yes, you are. We have two weeks left. Don't tell me you want to quit now." Ricardo stood up and threw some pants and a shirt on.

"What's the point? Mom is dead. I hate school."

"I'm not letting you quit. Do you want to end up like your mom? She had a terrible life, always trying to make ends meet." Ricardo pulled him up with one hand and set him on his feet. "This is about your life and what you're going to accomplish. You're the smartest kid I know."

"It's two weeks, then four more years, and who knows what after that?"

"Wait, four years? Did you get accepted?"

"Yes, the University of Idaho. But I can't go. I got accepted the same day my mother died."

"Like you said to me, if you don't go, I'll beat you. Except, I can do it. Now come on. Let's get breakfast and get on the bus."

Austin knew he had no options. He sighed as he put his shoes on. As they boarded the bus, he sat down next to Ricardo. "She talked to me on the way home yesterday."

"Who?"

"The gorgeous girl. Her name is Lisa. That's about all I know. I asked a question about the man she was staying with and she said to never ask again, then she left."

"Wow, that's awesome but weird. What do you suppose is going on?"

"I don't know. She says she'll be waiting for me to walk by again tonight. I just don't know. I don't have a reason to be in that neighborhood. I don't live there anymore. And now with Mom dying."

"Just walk by. What can it hurt? It might even cheer you up."

"I'll think about it."

When they arrived at school, Austin raced off to class. Unlike his bus, Ricardo's barely made it to school in time. As he sat in first period, the assistant principal stood at the door. "Gilbert, can I see you in the office?"

Everyone looked around to see who Gilbert was until Austin stood up and followed the vice principal out the door. When they arrived at the office, the principal sat behind his desk. His secretary and two assistants had joined him in there.

"I'm so sorry to hear about your mother passing away. If you need to take a few days off, I'll understand."

"Where would I go? I'm staying at Ricardo's house. His mom wouldn't want me underfoot. The police officer didn't like my living conditions. I might as well go to school. I can at least stay busy."

"If that's what you want. Again, you have our condolences."

The secretary and the vice principal patted him on the back on the way out of the office. During the breaks between classes, several girls came and hugged him, saying how sad they were to hear he lost his mom. He had never even seen some of them before.

When lunch came, Austin grabbed his food in time to see Ricardo pointing at him while talking to yet another girl. She came up and kissed him on the cheek. "I'm sorry for your loss."

He sat down next to Ricardo. "It's you who's sending all these girls my way and telling the principal."

"Someone told the principal. Dude, that wasn't me."

"How about all the girls?"

'That was me. I'm just trying to cheer you up, little buddy."

"There's only one girl I'm interested in."

"You can't limit yourself like that. I know in ninth grade I thought I met the love of my life in Emma Rodgers. Then her family moved away and I was heartbroken. Turns out, there are a lot better girls out there and she had done me a huge favor by moving away."

"Except for today, no other girl has given me a sideways glance."

"Yes, but you don't want to try for a goddess for your first one. They're usually stuck up and just playing with you for fun. You want to go with the simple girl. Cute, but not that much into herself. Those are the ones I have had the most fun with. It's the beauty queen type that every guy in school is chasing that you want to avoid."

"Gee, I hope she's not toying with me. Do you think she is?"

"I don't know. I've never met her. I do have to say is, near the end of the game, when you're down seven points, the quarterback heaves the ball into the end zone because he has nothing to lose, sometimes he ends up scoring. It's worth a shot."

"I never even told Mom about the girl. Now I regret that. She did know I was accepted to U of I. So, at least she knew about that." He put his fork down. "I can't eat."

"Sure, you can." Ricardo took a forkful of Austin's food. "Open wide."

"Really?" Austin grabbed his fork back.

"Just take that one bite, and then another and another. It starts out with the first bite."

"Fine." Austin stuffed the fork full in his mouth. "It looks like spaghetti but tastes like Chinese. It isn't so bad, though." He took another forkful.

At the end of school, Austin walked out of the weight room with Ricardo. "I don't know why I keep doing this. All my muscles hurt."

"That's because you weren't using them before. It gets better."

"I hope so."

"Are you going to see the goddess tonight?"

"Yes, she'll be waiting for me."

"I wish you luck, little buddy."

Chapter Eight

Austin slowed down as he rounded the corner. He hesitated under the tree, but he didn't hear anything. Heaving a sigh, he turned around.

"There you are. I didn't think you were coming," Lisa said. "You look so sad today. What's the matter?"

"Sorry, I didn't mean to look sad, it's just… my mother passed away yesterday. I mean, it wasn't totally unexpected, but it hurts anyway."

"Poor you." She hopped down from the tree and put her hands up to the fence. "I would hug you if I could, but hold my hands anyway."

He put his hands up against hers. The chain links and slats prevented them from interlocking fingers, but they could touch each other. "This feels good."

"You didn't tell me your name yesterday."

"Hi, I'm Austin."

"That's a great name."

"Thank you. I like your name, too."

"Oh, Lisa? Don't get too attached to it. I can't tell you any more than that."

"Interesting." Austin smiled, but then his eyes went, "Uh, oh. Your father." The man came out of the house pointing a pistol at Austin. He didn't need to raise his hands. They were already in the air touching Lisa's.

Austin stepped back. Four policed cars coming from both sides of Honeysuckle Avenue converged on him. He kept his hands in the air.

He could hear Lisa screaming at the man from the house. "Why did you do that? He's my boyfriend. We were just talking."

"You were standing there with your hands in the air. What was I supposed to think?"

"Oh, you!" She stomped off into the house.

"Get on the ground," one of the officers ordered. Austin complied. Soon they had him in handcuffs and stuffed in the back of a patrol car. His head reeled. *What did I do? Bank robbers don't get this much attention. Why does her dad, or whoever that guy is, have a gun? Did she say, boyfriend?*

As Austin sat there, he watched as one of the officers talked through the fence to the guy at Lisa's house. It looked to Austin as if the guy was giving orders to the officer, not the other way around.

Soon, he was whisked away to the police station. He passed Officer Fruean on the way to the interview room. They set him down and then shut the door. Austin sat there, staring at the walls. His hands cuffed behind his back.

Fruean stopped, turned, and watched them put Austin in the interview room. When the officers came out, he said, "I know that kid. What's he in for?"

"A real trouble maker, huh? He was harassing the W.P. girl."

"No, he's a good kid. His mother just died yesterday."

The other officer's eyes widened. "I don't get it then. Why'd the Marshal Service guy call us?"

Fruean walked into the observation room. He watched the pathetic Austin sitting there. Shaking his head, he walked into the interview room and unlocked the handcuffs. "There, is that better?"

Austin rubbed his swollen wrists. "Why am I here?"

"I don't know yet, but I'll figure it out for you. Hold tight."

When he left the room, the Marshal Service man stood there going through Austin's personal effects. *Goose. What a strange name.* He didn't like the guy. "We have Austin in interview one."

"Who is this kid? He's a ghost. I have no information on him. No driver's license, no car keys, only a house key, and student id card." He held it up. "Do you know how easily this is to forge? His fingerprints aren't on file, either."

"Let me fill you in then. He's lived his whole life here in town. The reason he doesn't have a driver's license is because he comes from a very poor family. My cousin has known that boy his whole life. In fact, he's staying at my cousin's house because his mother died yesterday."

The marshal looked up. "You're vouching for the kid?"

"Yes, I am. What did he do anyway?"

"That's Marshal Service business." Goose walked away.

"I'm going to listen in on this," Fruean told the sergeant.

"Be my guest. I don't like those guys anyway."

Goose sat down across from Austin. "You've been a busy boy. How do you know Lisa, anyway?"

"I stop and talk to her on the way home. She normally hides in the tree, so you won't see her. This time she came to the fence because my mom passed yesterday and she was trying to hold my hands through the fence."

Goose wrote a note on his tablet. "She's done this before?" Goose shook his head. "Where's home?"

"Around the corner. It was anyway, until yesterday. Officer Fruean wouldn't let me stay there anymore. I stay at the Fuimaono's now with my friend Ricardo."

Writing some more, Goose looked up. "Stay away from the girl or I'll shoot you."

Austin stood up and leaned over the table. "I didn't do anything wrong. Talking to her isn't a capital offense. Go ahead and shoot me. My life can't get worse, anyway." Austin's voice went up with every word. "I lost my mom, now I can't talk to Lisa. Shoot me now. why wait? You'd be doing me a favor."

Way to go, Austin, Fruean smiled to himself.

Two officers rushed into the room, but Goose put up his hand to stop them. "I'm done here. You're free to go, Gilbert, or Austin, whatever your real name is."

Chapter Nine

Ricardo's mom sat in the waiting room of the police station. She stood up when Austin walked out. "That girl is nothing but trouble."

"Tell me about it. How did you know I was here?"

"Half the town knows you're here. They were not subtle when they arrested you. Brandon called me to pick you up. He would have driven you home, but he's super busy today."

"Brandon?"

"You know him as Officer Fruean. You must be starving. I've got dinner in the oven."

"I am a little hungry. I've never been arrested before. I don't know why I was. I was just talking to Lisa."

"You have to forget about her."

I can't.

Austin followed her out to the car.

She stopped at the grocery store to grab a couple of items. Austin decided to wait in the car. He looked at the handicapped spot where he saw his mother alive for the last time. A tear dripped down his face. *Was that only yesterday? It feels like years ago. Poor Mom.* He wiped the tear away when the back of the car opened and Mrs. Fuimaono put the groceries in there.

When she sat down, she said, "I'm making Panipopo for dessert. You always loved my Panipopo. It will cheer you up."

"Thank you. I love that stuff."

As they passed the back of Lisa's house, he saw the U.S. Marshal standing in the back yard cooking at the grill like nothing had happened. This man helped turn Austin's world upside down but his life went on without a hiccup.

Ricardo's mom headed into the kitchen with her groceries in hand when they arrived at the house. Austin sneaked into his room and sat down. His backpack lay on the bed and he toyed with the idea of doing his homework, but he had all weekend to do that. He put the backpack off the bed and laid down. Closing his eyes, he tried to forget the last two days.

"Little buddy, how did it go with the girl?"

He opened his eyes to see Ricardo standing over him. "Not well. The cops arrested me for talking to her."

Ricardo laughed. "No, really, how did it go?"

"I'm not kidding. Your mom brought me home from the police station just now. They arrested me and took me into one of their interrogation rooms. The guy from the Marshal Service threatened to shoot me if I ever talk to the girl again."

Ricardo's jaw dropped open. "Dude." He sat down on the bed across from Austin. "What were the charges? Are you okay?"

"They never said what the charges were."

"Don't they have to tell you?"

"I thought so."

Ricardo left the room but came back a few minutes later. "My mom talked to Brandon. They didn't arrest you but just brought you in for questioning. Brandon said you stood up to the Marshal. He's so proud of you."

"Really? That's cool."

"What did you do?"

"He threatened to shoot me if I visited the girl again. I said go ahead, or something like that. I've had such a terrible week. I didn't care if he shot me or not."

"Wow, that's so awesome. Dude, listen, I wouldn't be intimidated by him. He's not going to shoot you in the middle of the street. I'd go right up to his house and knock on the door. I'll go with you if you want."

"Nah. It was just me reaching for the stars. I should have known better. Like your mom says, that girl's nothing but trouble."

Ricardo smiled, "She says that to me about every girl I date. We're going over to your mom's trailer tomorrow to clean it out. My mom contacted the landlord. He says you were behind in the rent, I guess. The landlord wants her stuff out now. We can see if there's anything worth saving. Maybe we can get you some extra money or something. You can hang out at the corner and see if the girl comes out."

"Are you sure he's not going to shoot me in the middle of the street?"

"He's in law enforcement. He's not going to shoot you without a good reason."

"What if he makes up something?"

Ricardo shrugged. "You worry too much, little buddy."

The next afternoon, Ricardo, his sister, and about six cousins approached the trailer. Austin unlocked it for them. "I'm sorry about my mother's room. It's a mess."

They all donned their gloves and masks and headed in. When Austin tried to walk in, Ricardo stopped him. "Go hang out at the corner. We got this."

Austin felt so obvious standing at the corner, occasionally walking back and forth. His heart sank when he saw the marshal watching him, then rolling his eyes. He took a step back when the door opened, ready to flee if he needed to. To his surprise, Lisa came out instead of the marshal. He ran across the street and up to the fence.

"Are you okay? I'm sorry that happened to you. Goose even feels sorry for you."

"He has a funny way of showing it. He threatened to shoot me."

"He threatens that a lot, but as far as I know, he's never done it."

"As far as you know?"

"I haven't known him that long. Forget about him. Tell me about yourself."

"Nothing much to tell. I grew up in town here. My mother raised me. She's been sick as long as I can remember. She finally died of whatever sickness she had. I don't know who my father is. My mother refused to tell me. I'd get one of those DNA tests, but I don't have any money of my own. I'm going to graduate in two weeks. That's about it. How about you? What's your story?"

She looked back towards the house. Goose was sitting on the back deck with his arms folded, glaring at the two of them. "Let's not talk about me right now. What's it like growing up in a small town?"

"It used to be a small town. It's been growing like crazy. I mean, traffic is so bad around here now."

She shook her head. "You have no idea."

Ricardo's cousin's truck drove up. "We're headed to the dump. Only found a couple of things that might have value. Hop in."

She smiled and waved, "See you later, Austin." She blew him a kiss.

"Bye."

Chapter Ten

"Hey, little buddy, looks like it's going well. She's cute."

"Yes, but that guy sat on the deck and glared at us the whole time," Austin replied.

"He didn't shoot you, did he?" Ricardo flashed him a smile.

When they arrived back from the dump, Ricardo spread out all the items they thought might be of worth, an old book, a couple of necklaces, and a music box. They also found a bunch of legal-type papers in an envelope. Austin picked up the music box. Winding it up, he let it play. "It still works. Mom used to play this for me when I was a kid." He held it as he watched the figurine slowly spin in a circle.

Ricardo slid the envelope over to him. "This stuff looked important."

Austin went through it piece by piece. "Wait. Here's a birth certificate, but it's not mine. It's a girl. Gwendoline Lena Morgan, born two years before me. It's lists Mom as her mother, and some Albert guy as the father." Austin leaned back on the couch. "I have a sister."

"Wow. Keep going. What else is in there?"

He pulled out another piece of paper. "It's a divorce settlement. It says this Albert guy gets sole custody of Gwendoline because the court ruled my mother as unfit. She didn't even get unsupervised visitation rights. The divorce was finalized seven months before my birth." Austin shook his head. "This is from the state of Florida. She must have moved out here to get away from him. I wonder why I never knew about my sister. She's was hiding me for some reason. That's why she used my middle name when sending me to school."

"How do you know that?"

"I'm speculating. Knowing my mom, I'm pretty sure I'm right."

"Wow. Does it have an address or anything?"

"I'm sure he's moved. My sister is probably in college by now. I don't know what to do," Austin said.

"Let's have some fun with this. Come on, let's check the computer." They searched for an Albert Morgan living in Florida. "Look. Here is someone by that name. He owns a car dealership in Miami. This could be the guy." Ricardo did a few more clicks. "Here's his picture. He does look like you."

Austin gazed at the picture of his older self. "Wow. Do you think he's the guy?"

"Look down here," Ricardo pointed. "It says his daughter, Gwen, works with him part-time while she's going to college. He's the guy."

"Wow, that's my father. What am I supposed to do with that information? He probably doesn't even know I exist."

"You don't know that. Call him."

"If he knows I exist, why hasn't he tried to find me?"

"Your mother hid well. How could he possibly find you? She had no assets. She didn't have a job. She didn't own property. She paid cash for the car because she couldn't get financed any other way. There was no way to locate her."

"Okay, you have a point. But what should I do? I can see it now. Hi, I'm Austin. I'm your son. Can I borrow some money for college?"

Ricardo laughed so hard he had to lean against the wall. When he caught his breath, he said, "Okay, we need to put more thought into that one. What else is in the envelope?"

Austin pulled out the last piece of paper. "It's a bank debit card. It can't have any money in it. Mom didn't have any money."

"Call them up and do a balance check. It's your money now. Even twenty bucks would help."

"Dinner's ready," Mrs. Fuimaono called from the kitchen. Austin stuffed the debit card into his pocket and went into the dining room.

Except for the plates, food took over the entire table. Ricardo, his two sisters, and his mother and father sat down. You always passed the food from left to right in their household or you would mess everything up. When a plate of food came along, Austin would hurry and put some on his plate because he knew that the next plate of food would arrive quickly after that. Like Ricardo, the whole family were large people and they took eating seriously. You passed the food quickly and you ate quickly. There were no family discussions at the dining table. That would come later. They would gather in the family room or around a fire in the wintertime, and tell how their day had gone. Austin would normally pass. He could get away with it most of the time, but no one was going to let him do that today.

Austin ate his fill, but that didn't stop Ricardo from putting a couple of extra pieces of meat on his plate. "Eat. You didn't take enough."

Austin tried, but he couldn't get it all down. Ricardo seemed satisfied, so he helped clear the table. The family gathered after they loaded the dishwasher. "Well, Ricardo, how did your day go?" the father asked.

"We helped clean out Austin's trailer. I'll let him fill in on what we found. It's so exciting. We took it to the dump and got rid of most of it."

"Hon, how did your day go?"

Mrs. Fuimaono smiled. "I applied for a couple of scholarships and financial aid in Austin's name. He didn't have a computer with internet at his house, so I did it for him. I had so much fun. I think he might even get one. It's a small one, but it will cover his housing while he's in school. The grants should cover the rest, I'm thinking, and if they don't, he can get a small student loan. Austin, you're going to college!"

"Thank you!" He stood up and hugged her. "Thank you so much." He swallowed hard. *Don't cry in front of the family.*

"Well, I guess we're all set now. Austin. How did your day go?"

"I don't know where to start."

"Start with the girl," Ricardo said.

"Oh, Lisa. I got to talk to her today. She's really nice and seems to like me. I wasn't much help to Ricardo and his cousins when they cleaned out the trailer."

"Tell them about the papers," Ricardo urged.

"Oh, I found my birth certificate. My mother was married when I was conceived. She divorced when she was pregnant with me. I know who my father is and I found out I have a sister."

The family clapped. One of Ricardo's sisters leaned over and hugged him.

"Tell them about the music box," Ricardo added.

"I should let you talk,"

"Go ahead, Austin." Ricardo's dad urged.

Austin took a deep breath. "I found the music box my mom used to use to put me to sleep as a child. It still works."

The family finished with their stories. Then the television came on and they watched a few of their favorite shows before bedtime arrived.

Austin snuggled down into the bed feeling loved. He had always loved spending the night at Ricardo's house. The family treated him like one of their own.

Austin had almost fallen asleep when Ricardo said, "I'm calling in the morning. I have the number."

"What?"

"I'm calling. I can't stand not knowing."

Austin sat up in bed. "Who are you calling?"

"I'm calling your sister. She works at the car lot. She should be there on a Saturday. That's when car lots are the busiest."

"What? No, you're not. I forbid it."

Ricardo chuckled. "We'll talk about it in the morning."

Wide-eyed, Austin stared at the ceiling the rest of the night.

Chapter Eleven

Austin searched for Ricardo's phone while he was in the shower. He knew it wouldn't stop him if he had the phone. Ricardo would borrow one of his sisters' phones. Still, it would slow him down. But then Ricardo came into the room holding up his phone, "Are you looking for this?"

"Please, don't."

"This is just a information gathering. We're going to find out if they know about you or not. That's all we're going to do. I was awake all night wondering about it."

"Right, that's why you snored straight through the last eight hours."

"Okay, maybe not all night. Here goes." He had already put the number in so he hit dial, then put it on speaker. "Hello, is Gwen Morgan there?" He waited a minute.

"This is Gwen."

"I have a friend named Austin. He thinks he might be related to you."

"What? Austin? Wait." He could hear her calling to her father.

"Honey, I'm busy with a customer."

"This person thinks he might have located Austin."

"Randall, can you take over for me? I have an emergency phone call."

Austin mouthed the word, "Wow!"

"Hello," the father's voice came over the phone.

"Hi, my name is Ricardo. My best friend is Austin Morgan. He saw his birth certificate for the first time in his life, yesterday. It lists you as the father."

"How can I contact him? What's his number?"

"He's right here listening in to the conversation. Here, I'll put him on." Austin shook his head vigorously. "Talk to the man. He's your father."

With a sigh, Austin took the phone but left it on speaker. "Hello, Sir. I don't mean to bother you at work. My mother passed away two days ago and we were going through her important papers and came across a divorce decree, a birth certificate for Gwendoline Morgan, and my birth certificate. I was wondering if the Albert Morgan listed on my birth certificate could be you."

"I'm sorry to hear about your mother. Just for identification purposes, what was her name?"

"Susan Lee Morgan."

"I want to meet you. Where are you at? I'll fly you out here."

"Fly me? I don't know about that. I've never been on a plane."

"You can bring your friend with you. Just come."

Ricardo nodded up and down. Austin replied, "We're in Idaho. The closest airport is in Spokane, Washington."

"Idaho? How did she end up there?"

"This is the only home I've ever known," Austin replied. "I graduate from high school in two weeks. I don't have a summer job yet, so I can come out after that."

"What high school do you go to?"

"It's called Lake City."

"Okay, let me know and I'll buy the plane tickets."

"Great. Wait, isn't it hot in Florida during the summer?"

Austin heard them laughing, so he guessed he was on speakerphone too. "We've survived it all these years. We have air conditioning. You'll be just fine."

"Oh, air conditioning, of course, you do. Thank you."

"Can I text my email to this phone? I'll have my secretary arrange the flight times."

Ricardo nodded so Austin said, "Yes."

"You have a good day. It's nice to finally hear from you, Son."

"Bye." Austin gasped. "He called me Son."

"I heard."

When Albert hung up the phone, Gwen asked, "Do you really think it's him?"

"I do. There is no way he could know about the money, so he's not after that. I'll have my doctor check for sure. But I'm convinced, it has to be him."

She wiped a tear. "It was so cruel of Susan to keep him from us all these years."

Sunday morning dawned bright. Austin jumped out of bed and dressed quickly. When he came out there on the table sat a note and a bowl of fruit. The Fuimaono family loved fruit for breakfast. The note said they had gone for a family drive up in the mountains. It made sense to Austin that they left him behind because otherwise, they would have had to take two cars.

He ate the fruit and walked out the front door. He locked the door after making sure the spare key was under the mat. He walked past the sign that said Private Community. The neighborhood wasn't gated, so he walked in like he belonged there. Walking over to the house he thought Lisa lived in, he hesitated. He couldn't tell from the back that the house was part of a duplex. He gave it his best bet and walked up and knocked on the door.

Goose opened it. "Oh, it's you."

Austin swallowed, but still asked, "Is Lisa here?"

"Listen, kid, you've got no chance with a classy girl like that. Why don't you go away and never come back?"

"But…" he stopped when Goose folded his arms. "Tell her I found my father. She might be interested."

"See you, kid."

Austin turned and walked off, dejected. *Classy girl? What did he mean by that? Maybe I'm a classy guy. He doesn't know.* Austin let go a huge sigh. *Maybe he does know. I'm a pathetic waif.* As he walked home, his head hung low.

Lisa came out of the shower in a bathrobe while drying her hair. "I thought I heard the door."

"Your not so secret admirer came over. I told him to get lost."

She stomped her foot. "I'm about done with all this isolation. I don't have to cooperate. If you keep me here in solitary confinement, I'll just go back home. You can't hold me. I didn't do anything wrong."

"All right." He held up his hands. "Next time Romeo comes over, I'll let him in."

"Good." She stormed off to her room and slammed the door.

He tentatively knocked on her door.

"What?"

"He said to tell you he found his father."

She threw the door open. "That would have been a wonderful thing to chat with him about. Now that moment is spoiled. I need to talk to him. You're a U.S. Marshal. Your job is to locate people. Find him." She slammed the door in his face.

Chapter Twelve

Austin waited until Monday to break the news to Ricardo. During lunch, he said, "The guy with Lisa told me to stay away. He said she was a classy lady and he didn't want a low life like me hanging around her. Okay, he didn't say low life, but he insinuated it."

"You're giving this guy too much power. You should go back there and try again. Let the girl say that to your face. Then you would know for sure."

Austin took a fork full of salad. "What if I don't want her to blow me off? Maybe she is a classy girl and I'm just a momentary distraction, someone to play games with. If I don't give her the chance to tell me to get lost, then I still have hope."

Ricardo shook his head. "Dude, that don't make any sense. If she's not the one, then go on to the next one. If she is the one, then she is the one."

"That's easy for you to say. With me, there might not be a next one."

Ricardo slapped him on the back. "You're just being plain silly now, Austin. You coming to weight lifting after class?"

"Sure. I had the weekend to heal. I don't hurt so bad."

"See you then."

On the way to his last class, two more girls hugged him and told him how sorry they were to hear about his mother. *Maybe there would be a next one. Is Lisa more trouble than she's worth?*

On their walk home, Ricardo talked about a girl he met on campus. A junior. He didn't usually date juniors, but he might make an exception this time. Austin half-listened while they walked. He waited for a pause, and then said, "Do you think I should give up on Lisa?"

"I can't answer that question. What does your heart tell you?"

Austin thought about it. "I don't know. My heart and my head keep arguing. I'm the guy stuck in the middle."

"Go with your heart."

"I know, but I don't want to face Goose again."

"Like I said, he's not going to shoot you in the middle of the street. There are rules against that."

"What if I go inside and he shoots me there?"

Ricardo shook his head. "Dude, you worry too much." Ricardo's phone beeped. He pulled up his email. "We've got tickets, little buddy. We're going to Florida!"

"When?"

"A week after graduation."

"I'm terrified of flying. Is it a small plane or a big one?"

"I'll check." Ricardo tapped a few times on his phone. "It's a 737, a small plane. It only holds a hundred and fifty or so people."

"A hundred and fifty? That's a small plane?"

"Yep." Ricardo checked the email again. "It's a red-eye. We'll be flying all night to get there." He smiled. "You can sleep through the flight, no worries."

"I don't know. I don't think I'll be able to sleep from now until the flight. I'm not liking this."

As they walked up to the house, Austin said, "I'm going to walk by my old house on the off chance she's in the back yard waiting for me."

"You go, guy. Just don't get shot."

"What?"

"I'm kidding."

Shaking his head, Austin headed up the street. He stopped at the tree she usually sat in and whispered, "Are you there?" Silence. He walked past the back of the house a couple of times, but she didn't come out. Sighing, he went around the corner. A construction crew sat in front of his old trailer. He watched as they took out pieces of the old floor and brought sheets of plywood in. His blood boiled. *How come you couldn't fix it while we lived there? I bet you even fixed the faucet in the shower.* As he stood there a carpet van pulled up. *You're even going to put in a new carpet!*

He walked past the back of Lisa's house a couple of more times.

Goose stood there watching out the window. Lisa walked into the room, "What are you looking at?"

"Your boyfriend walking back and forth along Honeysuckle Avenue. It looks like he's given up now."

"Why didn't you tell me?" She ran out the back door. "Austin. Austin." Peeking over the fence she couldn't see him." With a sigh, she came back into the house. "Why didn't you tell me?"

"You were busy with homework. That's more important."

"I could have taken a break. You don't get the picture, do you? Let me explain it again. I'm just about to give up on this whole adventure. If I don't have someone to talk to soon, I will. Now, what direction did he go? I want you to get in your car and track him down. I'm going with you."

They drove up and down Honeysuckle, then Ramsey. They even looked up and down highway ninety-five, but they couldn't find him. As they walked back into the house, Goose apologized. "Next time, I'll go get him."

She glared. "If there is a next time. I'm surprised he even tried after you told him to get lost. What have you done to find out where he lives?"

"He used to live right around the corner until his mother died. I see now they're remodeling the place, so I assume he doesn't live there anymore. I can't find out where he is now. I'm assuming he's staying with friends. One of the officers at the stationed mentioned something about him staying with his cousin, but I don't remember which one it was. The cops all look the same to me. I do know he's a senior so he'll be graduating in less than two weeks."

"Can we go?"

"I'll have to call in more security, but we'll try."

She smiled. "Thank you."

Chapter Thirteen

"Well, how did it go, Romeo?" Ricardo asked.

"If I remember my Shakespeare right, he didn't end up with the girl in the end. It's looking to be a Romeo do-over as she didn't come out. Maybe she's given up on me."

Ricardo shook his head. "Or maybe she went shopping. Dude." He walked over to the table. "Let's forget about her for right now anyway." He put his textbook down. "It's finals and I need your help."

Austin grabbed his book and sat across from Ricardo. "Okay, let's start with the Magna Carta."

Ricardo grimaced. "I hate history."

"Really? I love it. It's my favorite subject."

Ricardo stayed after, but Austin headed home right after school. He hadn't asked Ricardo which bus he should take so he decided to walk. He felt someone watching him. When he looked back, Koot and his gang were following him. He quickened his pace, but they ran up on him. Surrounded, he stopped. "What do you want? I don't have any lunch money."

"You disrespected me," Koot said. "You don't have Ricardo walking home with you to protect you. Now you're going to have to pay." He squared off to Austin and raised his fists.

Not wanting to get hit first, Austin slugged him in the gut. Koot doubled over with an "Oof."

Turning, Austin walked away. No one followed. *Wow, that weight lifting is really helping. I should have stayed today.*

As he arrived at Ricardo's house, he thought about going over to Lisa's but decided against it. He studied for his last two finals then it would be over. Twelve years of going to public school would come to an end. He pulled out his class schedule for the U of I. Flipping through it for at least the one-hundredth time, he scanned the classes he had circled. *A Vandal. I've never been a Vandal before. Mom always told me not to Vandalize.* He snickered at his own joke.

Ricardo walked in the door a minute later. "Thanks for the help in Social Studies. I think I did well. If I didn't, well, I only need to get fifty percent on the final to get a C in the class."

"Never aim for a C. Always try for an A."

"I know. You keep telling me that, but I'm not as smart as you are. By the way, I heard you punched Koot in the gut. Well done."

Austin creased his forehead. "How did you hear about that?"

"Derick told me. He said Koot's a wimp if you can take him. He and Garth won't be hanging around him anymore."

"Oh, no, I broke up the Koot gang." He let go a laugh.

"Good job. Listen, can I get your graduation tickets? I have a lot of family coming in for it."

Austin shrugged. "I guess. I'll keep one just in case I have the guts to invite Lisa."

"Sure, Dude, Thanks. Are you going over to see her today?"

"I'll go tomorrow. I want to give Goose time to learn to be nice."

Ricardo shook his head. "From what my cousin in the police force says, that's not going to happen."

"I'll go tomorrow anyway. It will give me a chance to get up my nerve." He sat down on the couch. "Do you think she's just playing with me?"

"No, but go see her. See what she does."

The next day, after weight lifting, he headed over there. Instead of walking back and forth at the back of her house, he marched past the private community sign and knocked on the front door. Goose answered. Sighing, he opened the door. "Come on in." Wide-eyed, Austin stepped through.

"Austin," Lisa ran out of the back room and threw her arms around him. "It's so nice you came to see me. Let's go into my bedroom and talk."

"Leave the door open," Goose replied.

"You're not my father." She slammed the door. "I heard about you finding your father. That's so exciting. Where does he live?"

He gazed around the room. *Am I really talking to her without a fence between us?* "Um, he's in Florida."

"Florida? Wow, that's a long way away. I had hoped he would live closer. Is he going to want you to come live with him to make up for old times?"

Austin shrugged. "I have no idea. I hadn't thought about that. I don't think I want to live in Florida. He has sent tickets for Ricardo and me to go there and visit him, but he hasn't said anything about me moving there."

"That's something you'll have to discuss with him, I'm sure. I know driving a moving truck across country isn't going to be that much fun."

"A moving truck." He smiled. "You can fit all my belongings in a small box."

"Really? A small box."

"I wish I was exaggerating, but I'm not. Mom and I never had much. She had a room full of junk, but that's all it was. We drove it all out to the dump after she died."

"Where do you live now? Goose says they're tearing your old house apart."

"Ricardo's family has taken me in." He pulled the ticket out of his pocket, "Before I forget, here is a ticket to my graduation. I want you to come."

She grabbed the ticket and hugged it to her chest. "I would love that. Thank you."

"Enough about me; let's talk about you. What year are you in school?"

"I'm going to graduate, too, but from on online school. I'll get a diploma, but no ceremony."

"Where are you from?"

She shook her head and then gazed down at the ground. "We can't talk about that. I'm sorry."

"What can we talk about? Where are you going to college?"

"If I get to go, well, I'm thinking about M.I.T. but I'm up to almost anywhere. I haven't decided yet. I want to major in engineering. I have a talent for taking things apart and fixing them. I fixed one of Goose's guns. It was jammed."

"*One* of his guns? How many does he have?"

"Lots. There is always one or two within easy reach. I even have a couple of them in my room in case." She paused. "In case of, well, never mind." She gave him half a smile. "How about you? Where are you going to college?"

"I've been accepted at U of I. I'm going to get an undergraduate degree in history, then go on to get my law degree."

"Cool, but isn't there a school nearby where you can do that? Isn't Iowa a long way away?"

"Iowa?"

"You said you were going to the University of Iowa."

"No," he smiled. "U of I around these parts means the University of Idaho."

She laughed, "Oh, that's silly of me. I guess you can tell I haven't been here long."

"Yeah, kinda. That's so neat that you might get to go to M.I.T. Do you think you'll be able to?"

She looked down at the ground again. "Well, I can't talk about that either."

Chapter Fourteen

Goose tapped on the door. "We have that appointment, Lisa."

She sighed, "I've got to go. Promise you'll visit me again."

"I will. We'll be headed for Florida soon, but after that."

As they stood up, she hugged him. "It's so nice to have someone to talk to."

"Yes, it is." He smiled back.

She showed the graduation ticket to Goose when they left the bedroom. "Look what I have."

He looked at it. "I'll need four more of these. We'll have to have tickets, too, to provide security."

"It's the only one I have left. I gave the other ones away."

Lisa's shoulders slumped. "You mean I can't go."

"I'll try to get more tickets," Austin replied.

Goose shook his head. "I should be able to work something out. Don't worry about it, kid."

Lisa watched Austin walk down the street. "You can't keep him," Goose said.

She turned. "Why not?"

"Let's see, he's going to college and you're not. You'll be going back home in a few months when this is all over. He'll be staying in Idaho. There are a lot of reasons."

"I don't know what my future holds, but I do know I like the guy." She sat down. "Just think, when you're rid of me, you can get your normal life back."

"I can't wait."

As Austin walked into the house, Ricardo smiled. "Dude, you look like you're on cloud nine. It went well, didn't it?"

"She talked to me and Goose didn't even shoot me."

"Did you give her the ticket?"

Austin's smile disappeared. "She can't go. I don't have enough tickets to cover her security detail."

"Do you need some back?"

Shaking his head, Austin replied, "I can't do that. You've already told your family members they could come. Goose said not to worry about it, whatever that means."

"I can tell the cousin I can't stand that you need the ticket back. I won't even mind."

"No, Goose said he would need four more tickets. Let's not worry about it. It's over."

"All right, Dude, but I'm glad the evening went well."

"Me too. I'm allowed to come back, too."

"Cool. When are you going back?"

"Probably after Florida. I have so much to do before that."

"I can't wait. I'm so excited to go."

"I have to bury Mom first. Your mother said the coroner called. They have released the body. They want to send it to a funeral home. I can't afford that."

"Let's go talk to Mom." He headed down the hall with Austin in tow. "Austin needs to come up with some money to bury his mom."

"I'll call around." She stood up and grabbed her phone off the table. An hour later, she said, "I found someone who'll do it for eighteen hundred."

"I can't afford that!" Austin clutched his heart.

"I know dear, but I can. You can pay me back someday, or not. I'm not worried about it."

"Thank you so much. I'll pay you back, I promise."

"Don't worry about it meanwhile."

"Thanks."

Two days later, when all the arrangements had been made, Austin found himself standing next to his mother's casket, cloth-covered and simple. He didn't want to view the body. He wanted to remember her alive. The whole Fuimaono family, including children and cousins, Austin's next-door neighbor, and the man who lived across the street from him, were the only attendees. Austin didn't have a formal funeral service, just the graveside reading of a couple of poems his mother had written.

He pulled out his last words to his mother, "Dear Mom. You were…" Choking up, he tried again. "Dear Mom," was all he could get out. He handed the paper to Ricardo.

"Dear Mom. You were always there for me. When I scraped my knee, you gave me hugs and kisses and a bandage. When I graduated kindergarten, you were the happiest mother there and you gave me hugs and kisses. You always supported me in my education. You always supported me no matter what I did by giving me your hugs and kisses. Now I'll never have another hug or kiss from you. That's the thing I'll miss the most. Your son, Austin."

The Fuimaono family sang "Amazing Grace". With one last touch of her casket, they walked away.

"Is that all there is for a whole life? A small eulogy when life is over? Only one son, one relative, to morn for you. She should have been surrounded by friends and family, a lot of family." When Austin stepped into the car, he looked back. "They're sticking my mother in the ground." *I shouldn't have looked back.* He shook uncontrollably and sobbed. Ricardo put his arm around him and Ricardo's sister patted his arm.

In the shadow of the nearby trees stood Goose and two other U.S. Marshals. Lisa peeked out from behind one. "Thanks for bringing me here." She nodded. "Poor Austin. He lost his mother in death." She sighed. "I'm putting my grandfather away for life. How's that any different?"

"He's a bad man. Austin's mom was a good woman. That's the difference."

Chapter Fifteen

With his mom's death certificate in hand, along with an affidavit to avoid probate, Austin walked into the bank. Going up to the counter, he said, "I'd like to withdraw my mother's account."

"Oh, I'm so sorry for your loss. Let me bring up her account. I'm going to send you over to Brad at the desk there."

He sat down across from Brad. "I'm so sorry for your loss," Brad said.

"Thank you. *" It sounds so insincere when I've heard the same phrase for the hundredth time.*

He typed a few more keys. "Yes, here it is. She has three hundred sixty-four dollars in it." Brad counted it out. "There you go. If you have any banking needs, we're here to serve you. Do you want to leave your account open? It looks like she had an auto-deposit once a month."

"No, close the account. Let whoever is depositing money in there will know she's passed away. Thanks again."

"Will do."

He sat in the car next to Ricardo's mother. He looked at the measly amount of money in his hands. *She didn't have enough to pay rent. It was all the pizza orders. Did she know she wasn't going to be around much longer?* He swallowed hard.

"Are you okay?"

He shook his head. "Three hundred dollars. It's not much to show for an entire lifetime. Do you want it to help pay for the funeral?"

"No, heavens, no. You'll be starting college soon. You'll need that to get settled."

He stuffed the money in his shirt pocket. Ricardo, in the back seat, patted him on the shoulder.

"I'm taking you and Ricardo clothes shopping. You need nice clothes to graduate in."

"Why?" Ricardo asked. "It will all be covered by our cap and gown."

"You won't be wearing your cap and gown for our party afterward. No, we're going."

The boys obeyed. When they arrived, Austin wondered why she had them try on several pair of pants and shirts. He'd never clothes shopped like this. Thrift stores were where his mother took him and they rarely had his size. They would buy one pair of pants, if that. Shirts were more adaptable. They could be a little loose or a little tight. That's what he wore most of the time. Rarely did he find one that he liked and fit him perfectly.

The boys arrived home with multiple pairs of pants, shirts, and socks. She even bought a new pair of shoes for Austin. He offered to pay her, but she didn't even respond, just shook her head. He worried about overstaying his welcome. Ricardo would tell him if there were problems. *Wouldn't he?*

"Austin, you think too much." Ricardo's words rang through his head.

He put his new clothes away in his box that sat on top of Ricardo's dresser. He was in the way and costing the family money. He would inquire about doing a summer term so he could stay on campus and be out of their hair. *What about Florida?* He shook the thought out of his mind. *They probably don't want me underfoot either. Besides, it's too hot.*

Ricardo walked into the room and slapped him on the back. "Well, little buddy, this is it. Just a few days and we'll be all graduated."

"Can't wait."

"Mom let me borrow the car. Do you want to get some burgers and fries at Rodger's? They have great malts there. Then I'll drop you off here. I have a date."

"Okay." Austin didn't love burgers as much as Ricardo did. "You're taking that girl out you were talking about the other day?"

"The junior? Yes. I'm making an exception to my only dating seniors rule with her. Come on, let's go."

As he walked out to the car, Ricardo asked, "Do you want to drive?"

"I don't have a driver's license."

"Your mother had a car. Why not?"

"She nursed the car along and didn't want a new driver to mess it up. Besides, I would have had to take lessons and pay for a license, both of which cost money and that's something we never had enough of."

"We have to fix that."

"No. I've encroached on your family enough. Let's just go. Besides, I'm trying to get into the summer term. I don't have time to complete driver's ed."

Ricardo hesitated for a minute, then sat down in the car. When Austin had gotten in, he said, "Don't think for one second that you're a burden by being here. I'm having the time of my life. I have a guy, my age, to talk to. I get tired of talking about women's stuff with mom and my two sisters."

Austin nodded. "Thank you. I needed to hear that."

After eating, Ricardo dropped him off. Austin walked into the house. Ricardo's sisters and mom were baking and making treats. "Do you want to help?" one of the sisters asked.

"I would love to."

"Don't feel like you have to. It's your party, after all."

"No, it sounds fun. This is a lot of food for the family, isn't it?"

Ricardo's mom laughed. "You don't have any idea how big our family is. Besides, we've invited friends, too. It's a good thing we've got a big backyard. I borrowed tables from all the neighbors. It's going to be a blast."

"I can't wait. Thanks for putting up with me."

"Of course. Why wouldn't we? I've liked you since the first time I met you. You're Ricardo's favorite, too. We love having you here."

"Thanks," He swallowed hard, but it didn't help. A tear formed in his eye. He turned his head to wipe it away, but one of Ricardo's sisters stood on that side of him and saw it.

"Are you okay?"

"Oh, just, um, eyes are itchy. Must be my allergies."

She gave him a half smile. "Sure, that must be it."

Austin waited until Ricardo came home before going to bed. "How was the movie?"

"Movie, oh yeah, the movie. It was okay, I guess." Ricardo smiled. "I think this girl is the one who might make me give up on all the other girls."

"She's the one? Austin asked.

"I think so. Only, she still has another year of high school left. But she wants to go to WSU too when she graduates."

"So, you only have to wait a year."

"Wow, a whole year. And I'm going to meet lots of new girls at college. Dude, now you have me all confused."

"Maybe it's not time to settle down?"

"Hmm., Maybe. I really like this girl, though."

"You can see her on the weekends."

That brought a big smile to Ricardo's face.

Chapter Sixteen

"Come on, boys." Ricardo's mom called through the bedroom door.

Austin and Ricardo were putting the final touches on their cap and gown. "No, the tassel goes on the other side until you graduate, then you move it over."

Ricardo grumbled, "Who made up all these silly rules?" He moved his tassel. "I mean men wearing gowns and the stupid flat hat that doesn't stay on my head too good."

"It's tradition."

Ricardo opened the door. "We're ready."

"Good, get in the car. You're supposed to be in your seats in the next half hour."

As they entered the gymnasium, the whole floor had row upon row of chairs for the graduates. The bleachers were filling up fast. "Wow," Austin said. "This is crazy."

"I wish they could have held this on the football field. I feel more at home there."

"This is going to be more people than the basketball games." They took their place in line. After getting their name IDs they sat down next to each other. Several girls sat down next to Ricardo as if they were waiting for him to sit first. One nearly sat on Austin's lap. "Excuse me."

"Oh, sorry." She moved over a little, but still crowded him.

Austin had to listen to a speech by the valedictorian who had only beaten Austin's grade point average by one-tenth of a percentage point. When the speeches were done, the graduates filed up to the stage. The administrators announced not to cheer for each individual graduate, but as a group. That didn't stop anyone, however.

Following Ricardo's thunderous roar of cheers, Austin figured the crowd would be dead silent when he walked across the stage. To his surprise, he heard small cheers from two different directions. He tried to see who cheered, but he couldn't isolate anyone in the crowd. He held his diploma high as he stepped off.

Sitting back down, the girl who had crowded him jumped in front of him in line to sit next to Ricardo. Austin didn't care. The ceremony would end soon after that. Leaving the auditorium, Ricardo was mobbed. Austin smiled as he stepped by Ricardo's family, some of whom he recognized.

Lisa stayed in the shadows until Austin came out. She stepped out, only to retreat when a girl threw her arms around Austin.

"Oh, competition," Goose said. "The boy has been holding out on you."

"He doesn't know who it is. He looks as puzzled as I am."

A man stepped up and shook his hand, vigorously. "I'm your father, Austin. We flew up to watch you graduate."

"Hi, I'm Gwen, your sister."

"Oh, wow. Hello."

Lisa turned to leave.

"You're not going to talk to him?" Goose asked.

"He's having a family moment. I'll leave him to it."

"All right. At least we were here."

His father and sister were at the graduation party. Austin wondered about it but didn't ask. Finally, Ricardo took pity on him. "Two of the tickets you gave me were for your father and sister. We've been corresponding this whole time behind your back. They wanted to surprise you."

"They did that. It would have been nice to have Lisa there, too."

"She was. I saw her in the crowd. She almost came up to you but retreated when she saw your sister run up and hug you."

"She was? She doesn't think Gwen is a girlfriend I didn't tell her about, does she?"

"I don't know. That was a great hug."

"Oh, no. I have to talk to her."

"Not for the next two weeks. Your father wants us to show him around our area, then we're off to Florida."

Austin opened his mouth to say something, but just then his father came up. "This is a great shindig, son. You live in a pretty area. I love the mountains all around. We don't have those in Florida. Some people describe us as a great big sandbar. The whole state, that is."

"Wow, I can't wait to visit."

"Coming up. Ricardo has told me all about your Rathdrum Mountain. We want to hike around it. Gwen is planning on packing a picnic lunch. Okay, we don't have a kitchen in our hotel room, but you do have a chicken place here in town. We'll let the Colonel do the cooking."

"Sounds fun." Austin pasted a smile on his face.

The music blared until late in the night. None of the neighbors complained though, since they were all at the party. Austin had time to talk to his sister between songs. She told him about her classes at the University of Miami where she majored in Marine Science. "It's Dad's alma mater."

"Oh. What did he major in?"

"Business."

Austin laughed. "I should have guessed that."

She put his hand on Austin's arm. "Do you have any pictures of Mom? I don't remember what she looked like. I was only two when she left."

"I have a few of her when I was a child. When she got sick, she wouldn't let anyone take pictures of her." He pulled out his wallet. "Here is my favorite. I'm four in the picture."

"She's so pretty."

"She looks a lot like you," Austin replied.

"No, I'm not pretty like her."

"Don't be silly. Yes, you are."

She blushed, "Thank you."

Ricardo sat down by the two of them. "Hi, I'm Austin's best friend. You must be Gwendoline."

"Yes, Ricardo. I guess you're coming out with Austin. That will be fun. Please call me Gwen."

"I can do that."

She gave him a huge smile. Austin's heart sank. *Another Ricardo admirer. How does he do it? All he did was say hi.* "I'm going to go mingle." He stood up and walked off.

"Great party, huh?" One of Ricardo's sisters bumped his arm. "Do you dance?"

"No."

"Great, I can teach you." She pulled him out into the middle of the lawn and began dancing.

Austin tried to mimic her moves but came up short. He looked around to see if anyone was laughing at him. Of those dancing around him, none were paying him any attention. Those on the sidelines were engaged in their own conversations. He relaxed and did his own thing.

After the dance, he rejoined the conversation with Gwen and Ricardo. *They're getting along well.* Ricardo's sister walked by but left him alone. When Gwen and Ricardo stood up to dance, his sister pounced and dragged Austin back out.

"You dance pretty good, little buddy," Ricardo commented on the way by.

Mr. Morgan came up to Austin after the dance. "I almost forgot. My attorney wants you to do a paternity test before he changes the will. I have a mouth swab if you're okay with that."

Nodding, Austin replied. "I understand the paternity test. I have no problem with that. In fact, I'm interested in the results also. As for the will, I'm not feeling good about that. Gwen has been with you the whole time. She should get everything. I'm just a Johnny-come-lately in your life."

"We can talk about that later. Here, swab this in your mouth." Austin did and Albert sealed it in the plastic bag and stuck it in the envelope. "Great, we should have the results by the time we get to Florida."

Chapter Seventeen

The hike up Rathdrum Mountain didn't go well. A morning rain stopped, but the trees still drizzled on the group. Mr. Morgan began heavy breathing nearly from the car. "It must be the altitude," he said.

Ricardo whispered to Austin, "We're only at about two thousand feet here. How's he going to handle the three thousand feet up ahead?"

"Look, it's Sasquatch." Gwen pointed to a statue at the beginning of the trail. "Go stand by it, Dad."

He caught his breath and stood by the statue. "Go over there with him. I'll take a picture of both of you," Austin volunteered.

"No, you're part of the family now." Gwen handed her cell phone to Ricardo. "Can you take a picture of our family?"

"Sure." They all smiled as Ricardo snapped their picture.

As they climbed, Albert needed more and more rest breaks. "Is the summit worth the climb?" he finally asked.

"This trail doesn't go to the summit. It's just a nice walk in the woods," Ricardo replied.

"What? I'm staying here. You guys go up ahead without me."

"But, Dad," Gwen protested. He held up his hand. "Okay. We'll go up but not eat lunch until we get back here."

"Sounds good."

As they turned the next corner, Austin stopped. "I'm worried about him. I don't think altitude sickness occurs at two thousand feet. It's more like ten thousand."

Ricardo pulled out his cell phone. "I'll check."

"You get reception way out here?" Gwen asked.

"Sure, there's a cell tower on the mountain." He clicked his phone a few times. "You're right, Austin. You can get it between five and eight thousand feet. It's more prevalent between eight and ten thousand."

"I vote we go back and take him to a walk-in clinic," Austin replied.

Gwen didn't say anything but turned and headed back down the trail. When they arrived back at the spot where Albert sat, he was still having trouble breathing. "We're taking you to a doctor, Dad."

"Why?"

"You're not well."

"It's the altitude."

"No, Dad, it's not." She helped him up.

After waiting forty-five minutes to get in, Mr. Morgan had another hour's worth of tests. When he came out, he sat down by the group. Smiling, he said. "I feel so much better. They gave me oxygen."

"What's the problem?" Gwen asked.

"The doctor called it dyspnea. He says the anxiety of coming out west for the first time and meeting my son could have brought it on. He suggests that I don't climb any more mountains until they're sure. They are waiting for some more test results. My EKG and blood oxygen levels are good, however."

Gwen hugged him. "I'm so glad it isn't anything serious."

"Me too."

"The chicken is cold by now. I say we go out to dinner. There's a Cracker Barrel by the freeway at the end of Ramsey. They have good fried chicken there."

"Let's do it. A nice restaurant sounds good."

When they arrived, Austin stepped out of the car and scanned the building. He whispered to Ricardo, "What are we supposed to do?"

"What do you mean?" he whispered back.

"Are you two okay back there?" Gwen asked.

Austin cleared his throat. "I'm sorry. I've gone to fast food places, but this is my first time at an actual restaurant. If I am doing the wrong thing, please kick me under the table."

"Sure, no problem," Ricardo replied.

"We're not kicking you under the table." Albert put his arm around him. "Just follow my lead." They walked in together.

Gwen stared after them. Ricardo creased his forehead. "What are you doing?"

Gazing up, she said, "He's never been to a restaurant before? What type of life has he had?"

"A very bad one. I haven't told him this, but we chased rats out of his mother's room when we cleaned out the trailer. She collected a lot of garbage over the years. We threw all of her stuff out except for a couple of items. The police wouldn't let him stay in the trailer because of the terrible conditions. That's why he lives with us now."

She shivered. "I guess I take too much for granted. Poor Austin. His life is going to change so much for the better in ways he can't even imagine."

"I'm so happy for him. I've been his friend since grade school but I didn't know until recently all the things he's gone through."

"Shall we go in?" she asked.

He offered her an arm and she took it.

"Well, you two are getting pretty chummy," Albert replied.

"He's just being a gentleman, Dad."

Austin scanned the menu. "Wow, all this food. I don't know what to order."

"Go with the fried chicken. You can't go wrong with fried chicken," Gwen replied.

"Okay, that sounds good. Who do I tell?" When the waitress came up, they all ordered fried chicken. Gwen helped Austin pick out some side dishes. They chatted until the food came out. Austin gazed down at the table, "Wow, it's a feast."

Chapter Eighteen

When they finally parked the car, Albert stepped out first. Taking a large breath of air, he smiled.

"Are you okay, Dad? If it's too high up, we can drive back down quickly." Gwen studied his face.

"I'm great. The doctor said I couldn't climb up mountains; he didn't say anything about driving up them. Look at the view from up here." It had been Albert's idea to drive up Mount Spokane. Gwen had tried to talk him out of it after the last episode, but he insisted.

"If you were going to have altitude sickness, this would be the place. You look better than you did on Rathdrum Mountain and it's twice as high here than where we stopped there," Ricardo added.

"Let's enjoy the moment. What are these tubes, Ricardo?" Gwen asked.

"You see what it tells you on the outside? You look down the tube so you can see what it's pointing to. This one says Lake Coeur d' Alene, for example. Then you look through the tube and you see the lake."

"That's cool. Have you seen this before, Austin?"

"He's probably been up here dozens of times," Albert commented.

"Nope, this is the first time. My mother's car wouldn't have made it up this far."

"Oh, but you've been here before, Ricardo."

"Yes, we came up last week as a family. I should have brought Austin. I didn't know he'd never been here before. We could have stuffed him in the car."

"Like in the trunk," Austin responded. "I was okay with not coming. You can't fit another person in that car of yours. Besides, you guys needed the family time."

Ricardo shrugged.

As they enjoyed the height, they walked up to the Vista House on top of the mountain. Albert looked down. "Wow, they ski down this? It's so steep."

"It's steeper on the other side," Ricardo replied.

"I'm never taking up skiing."

When Austin had Ricardo alone, he said, "I haven't had a minute to sneak over to Lisa's place and tell her that Gwen is my sister and not my love interest."

"I don't think that's going to happen today either. We're all going to the steak house tonight, your family and my family, then we're leaving tomorrow, early."

Austin sighed. "My first girlfriend and I lose her to a simple misunderstanding."

"Relax. As soon as you get home, I'll let her know all about it. You won't have to worry."

Austin nodded. "Okay, thanks." He looked over at his father and sister. "How can someone have so much money? He's taking us all to dinner. It cost over fifty bucks to eat lunch yesterday. I saw the ticket. It's going to be twice that tonight."

"It's going to cost more than twice that. The steak house is a lot more expensive. But don't worry. Fifty dollars isn't that much. I think your dad has lots more money than you think he does. He's not going bankrupt any time soon."

Austin shook his head. "I'm not saying that. It's a lot of money to be spending on one meal. He could buy two weeks' worth of groceries for what he's going to spend tonight."

"Maybe a month's worth. Just go with it."

Sighing, Austin walked over to Gwen and Albert at the Vista House. "This is so beautiful," Gwen said.

"Yes, it is." Albert agreed.

Gwen leaned over to Austin and said in a low voice. "Before we go to dinner, I want you to take me to Mom's grave. I barely remember her, but she is still my mother."

"Sure, we'll head there right after this."

When they were done exploring and taking pictures, they hopped in the car and headed down the hill. Austin and Gwen sat in the back. "Are you on Facebook?" She asked.

"I've heard of it."

"Oh, maybe you can get Ricardo to set you up."

Ricardo smiled. "He didn't even have a tv at his house, but he did well in keyboarding and spent a lot of time in the computer lab at school, so he knows how to use a computer."

Austin smiled. "I saw two people typing each other on this online dating site. What they didn't know was that, in real life, they were sitting right next to each other. I sat in the row behind them so I could see what they were doing. The really funny thing is, neither one of them matched their online profile picture. You see a lot of interesting things in a computer lab." His smile disappeared when they crossed the border from Washington to Idaho. "Take exit five."

"Exit five?" Ricardo asked. He turned to see Austin. "Oh, I know where we're going. Yes, take exit five, then head north." When they arrived at the cemetery, Ricardo said, "Turn right here."

They parked close to the grave and stepped out of the car. A simple marker with her name on it stood out of the top of the fresh grave.

Tears dripped down Austin's cheeks. "I only went to get groceries. She was alive when I went into the store."

Gwen put her arm around him. "I shouldn't have made you bring me here."

"No, I needed to come, too."

"Is there a headstone coming?" Albert asked.

"No," Ricardo answered. "This is it. We were going to do all that, but Austin didn't want us to. He's going to pay us back someday and didn't want to run up the bill too far."

"I'll pay you back and get her a proper headstone. I spent four years of my life as her husband. I owe her that much at least."

Chapter Nineteen

Auston swallowed hard as they sat in the airport terminal. A happy Gwen announced, "That's our plane," as it pulled up to the jetway.

He kept peeking at it out of the corner of his eyes. *How does something that weighs so much fly?*

Gwen patted his hand as if she sensed what concerned him. "Don't worry, Ricardo and I changed seats. I'll be next to you the whole way. Dad and I fly all the time. You've got this."

Austin nodded, but then he frowned. "Isn't your father going to be unhappy with Ricardo sitting next to him? You see how big his shoulders are?"

"That will be a surprise for later. I didn't want to see you squished in a corner on your first flight. I like Ricardo, but I don't want to be stuck next to him, either. Dad will forget what happened in a day or two."

Austin snickered.

"Grab your bag. We're boarding."

Austin enjoyed having his sister next to him. She explained about takeoff and how he would be pushed back in his seat when they took off. She told him when to sleep and when the snacks and drinks were on the way.

"How was your childhood?" Austin asked at length.

"Oh, it was wonderful. Dad and I worked together. I sold cars for years. When I started school, he put me in the office on weekends so his office staff can have the weekends off. It works out perfectly for me. If it's slow at the lot, I'm even allowed to work on my homework."

"You said you flew a lot. Where do you go?"

"We've gone to Europe, Hawaii, and South America. We even took a few cruises."

"Wow. I couldn't even get up Spokane Mountain. Mom's cars were all second-hand. Or more likely fifth- to tenth- hand. She couldn't afford any better than that. The few times she put some money aside, the car would break down and she would have to buy a new one or get the old one fixed."

"You won't have to worry about that. You can have any car you want from off the lot. Except for the new ones, and if you sweet talk him, you might even be able to swing one of those."

Austin sighed. "I don't even have a driver's license."

"We'll fix that."

"Wow." He strained to look out the window.

"What can you see?"

"Tops of the clouds mostly. Every once and awhile I can see little ribbons with moving dots. Cars are really small from up here."

"Yes, really small."

"Do you want to trade places so you can look out the window?"

"No. I don't like the middle seat, and you need to look out the window. It's your first flight."

"Thank you." He gazed out again. "Oh, there's a river. Which one do you think it is?"

She pulled up the flight tracker on the video screen on the back of her seat. "Oh, it looks like the Mississippi. That was a good spot."

He leaned back in his seat. "Did your dad, er, I mean our dad... Did he date anyone else?"

"A couple. It's hard for a single dad. A lot of women don't want to raise someone else's kid."

"How about you? Do you have a boyfriend?"

"Wow, you're asking a lot of questions all of the sudden."

He blushed. "I'm sorry. You don't have to answer that."

"No, it's okay. I did have a salesman with a crush on me. He couldn't sell cars, so Dad fired him. He didn't come back around after that. I have other men that I've dated, but nothing serious. How about you? Do you have a girl back home?"

"I think so. I don't know. She came to graduation but disappeared when she saw you run up and hug me. I haven't had a chance to tell her that you're my sister."

"Oh, no. Give me her phone number and I'll call and explain everything to her."

"I don't have her phone number. I never had a phone so I didn't have need for phone numbers. In fact, I'm pretty sure she doesn't have a phone."

"She doesn't have a phone?"

"It's complicated."

"Is she poor like you?"

"Um, er, I don't know. I don't think so. We've never talked about it. She seems to have everything she needs. I'm not positive, but I'm pretty sure her family has money."

"How much do you really know about this girl?"

"I know she's pretty and smart. She has a great sense of humor and I know her name. I don't think it's her real name, but she doesn't talk about herself at all. She's my mystery woman."

"I guess." Gwen giggled. "Good luck with that."

"I know, it probably won't last, but I love being with her so I overlook all the secrets."

"Ahh, that's so sweet." She lowered her voice. "Does Ricardo have a girlfriend?"

"Only every girl in school."

She laughed.

Ricardo turned his head. "Is Austin telling stories again?"

"Yes, big ones," she replied.

The pilot announced the fasten seat belt sign was on and to prepare for landing. Austin looked out the window. "I thought there would be water. I've never seen the ocean before."

"Oh, this isn't Miami. This is Atlanta. We have to land and change planes. Then we'll go on to Miami."

A wide-eyed Austin said, "We have to do this again?"

"We get to walk around first, and this time we don't have to go through security."

"That's good. I didn't like that part."

Chapter Twenty

When they landed, Albert led them to the next gate. He stood and talked to the gate agent for a long time and then came back to the group. "We're all flying first class this last leg of the trip. I can't handle being in the middle seat when Ricardo is on one side and another large man is on the other. I felt like an Albert sandwich except the bread was in the middle and the meat was on both sides."

"Dad, that wasn't nice," Gwen scowled.

"Oh, sorry. No offense, Ricardo."

Ricardo laughed. "None taken. I have a mirror; I know how big I am. Thanks for being a good sport as long as you were."

The second leg of the journey went much better for Albert. Again, Gwen sat by Austin. At first, he looked out the window, but soon gave up. "It's dark. I'm still not going to see the ocean."

"I'll take you to South Beach tomorrow. You do swim, don't you?"

"Yes. My mom took me to Hayden Lake and Lake Coeur d'Alene as a kid. That was our vacation from the heat in the summertime. We didn't have air conditioning and the trailer would get so hot. She taught me to swim. We'd have so much fun."

"That does sound nice. The saltwater will be a bit different than you're used to, but it just means that you'll have to take a shower afterward."

He nodded. The plane started its descent and he grabbed the arm rests.

"The scary part isn't for a few minutes; you can relax."

"Oh, yeah, huh." He let go of the armrests. They chatted so much that the plane touched down before he realized it was close. "Oh, it's over."

"You survived your first airplane ride."

"Yes, but I still have the return flight."

She wrinkled her forehead. "Oh, you're going back? I thought Ricardo was returning by himself and you were going to stay with us this summer."

"I hadn't heard that. I thought I was going back."

"Don't worry, we'll send for your stuff."

"All my stuff fits into the suitcase your father, er, *our* father bought me. It's not that, it's, well, I have a girl."

"We'll figure out a way to face time with her. We've got this."

Austin folded his arms and looked forward. *You can't face time with her, the marshall Service won't allow it.* He watched out the window as the plane taxied up to the terminal. *I don't want to stay here all summer. I'll lose Lisa if I do.*

Cars seemed to be everywhere, all traveling down the highway at breakneck speeds. Austin had never seen anything like it. He could tell even Ricardo didn't like it either because he shifted in his seat often. Gwen and Albert seemed oblivious to the danger. When the rain began, it wasn't like an Idaho rain. The drops were half dollar size. Soon he could no longer see the lines on the roads, but that didn't slow Albert down or even any of the rest of the cars out that night.

"I'm sorry you didn't get to see our normally sunny state on a good day." Gwen tapped her father on the shoulder. "I forgot to tell you that Austin wants to go to the beach tomorrow."

"That's a great idea. I won't be able to come, but have fun."

"Can I come, too?" Ricardo asked.

"Yes, of course."

Albert turned a corner and stopped in front of a gate. He punched in some numbers into a key code and the gate opened to let him in. When they pulled into the driveway, Austin scanned the house. He had seen an apartment buildings smaller than this. "Does anyone else live here?"

Gwen giggled. "It's not even as big as some of my friends' houses."

"Oh."

"Hey, this place is cool," Ricardo said.

White tile floors greeted them as they walked in. Wrought iron handrails followed the steps up to a second-story loft. Sliding glass doors surrounded the pool on three sides in back and the pool itself had black netting around it.

"Your rooms are in the back." Gwen led the way.

"Rooms?" Austin asked.

"We have a two-bedroom guest house on the main level. It's off the kitchen, so you can sneak snacks during the night. Dad had his secretary stock the fridge with fresh food for you guys. It looks like Ricardo might have a big appetite, so we had her lay in extra." She opened the fridge on the way by to show them. She also showed them the pantry. "Help yourself to anything. If we run out, the grocery store isn't far away."

She turned the corner and opened the door. "Here is your room, Ricardo. Go ahead and put your things away in the dresser if you want. There is a bathroom with a shower next door. You two will have to share it, but you're guys, so that shouldn't matter." Ricardo stepped into his room. She led Austin past the bathroom to another door. "This is your room. It's only temporary while Ricardo's here, then you'll move into the spare bedroom upstairs next to Dad's and my rooms. Dad has to clean it out first and get some furniture in there. He might even let you help pick the furniture out. Anyway, good night."

"Good night." He smiled, but his heart screamed, *I'm being kidnapped.* He put his suitcase in his room.

Ricardo came out and tapped on the door. When Austin opened, he said, "Shh. Come here." Peeling back the curtain from the side of the hall, revealed a sliding glass door onto the pool. "What do you say we go for a plunge?"

"I outgrew my swimsuit. To tell the truth, it never fit well, to begin with."

"That's okay, I forgot to pack mine."

"What?" Austin gave him a sideways glance. "What are you suggesting?"

"They're asleep by now."

"It's only been ten minutes."

"I read somewhere that people fall asleep faster in the southern states. Come on." Before Austin could respond, Ricardo stripped naked, slid the door open, and hopped into the pool.

"Why do I listen to you?" Austin followed him in. *Maybe if I'm naughty, they'll send me back.* As they swam around, he confided in Ricardo. They think I'm staying. I don't want to stay."

"Albert bought round trip tickets for both of us. Why do they think you're staying?"

"Gwen keeps saying it. She says things like, I'll be moving upstairs after you go back to Idaho."

"Dude, that wasn't the arrangement. I'll talk to him."

"No, I'll talk to him. He may be my father."

The back light lit up the pool area and Gwen stepped out. "What are you two doing?"

"We're just swimming," Ricardo smiled, but they both headed to the side of the pool so the edge would hide them.

"What are you wearing?"

"I don't have a swimsuit. This was all Ricardo's idea."

"I forgot my swimsuit," Ricardo said. "Come join us."

"No way. It's too late to be swimming anyway. Come on, get out."

Ricardo shook his head. "Not with you standing there. Turn your back."

She did, but when he was halfway to the door, she said, "Oh my."

"You peeked," he snarled.

"Please don't peek this time. I'm your brother."

"You have a point. I promise." She closed her eyes.

He ran into the house.

Chapter Twenty-one

Mrs. Fuimaono answered the knock on the door only to be surprised when the man flashed his law enforcement badge. "Hello, Ma'am. I need to speak with Austin Morgan."

"He isn't here. He's gone to Florida with my son to see his father."

Lisa stepped out from behind a tree. "When will he be back?"

Goose held up his hand towards Lisa. "I said I'd handle this." Turning back to Ricardo's mother, he asked. "Do you know when he'll be back?"

She answered Lisa, not Goose. "They're scheduled to come back Wednesday, but Ricardo says Austin's father wants to keep Austin down there."

Lisa hung her head. "Thank you." She walked back towards the car. "Tell him I love him," she said right as she sat down.

"Thank you, Ma'am, for your cooperation." Goose walked to the car as did two more agents who came from each side of the house.

She picked up her phone and called Ricardo.

Austin walked into the kitchen as his father was reading the paper and sipping a cup of coffee. "Good morning." He pushed the paper over to Austin. "This ad of mine doesn't pop. What do you think it needs?"

Austin sat down and studied the ad. "All the cars say the same thing. Low mileage, one owner. Maybe if you put them in categories. These are our low mileage cars and these are our one-owner cars. The phone number is in the fine print at the bottom of the ad. It should be in huge letters at the top. You do want them to phone you. If they see it at the top before anything else, that's what they'll think about the whole time they're looking at your ad. Also, the pictures of the cars are from too far back. They need to be closer so you can see the car's details."

Albert took the paper back. "Wow, you're amazing. That's spot on. I'll have you start in the ad department when you come to work for me."

"About that. I was hoping to go back with Ricardo. I start school in the fall at the University of Idaho. I wanted to spend my last summer there. Besides, we don't know for certain if I'm even your son."

Albert slid over a letter. "Yes, we do. The paternity test results are back. It's a hundred percent certain. You're my son."

Austin picked up the letter. "Wow, I have a father! I've always wanted one of those."

"Your family is here, Son. You have a home, a father, and a sister. You'll have a car as soon as you pick one out. I have lots of pull at my old alma mater, the University of Miami. Even if your grades were bad, we can work something out. You don't have anything there."

"I have a girl."

Albert leaned back in his chair. "I see." He scratched his chin, then sipped his coffee. "I want you here. How about, you go back with Ricardo and stay a month, then come to live with me?"

"How about the whole summer? Meanwhile, we can discuss the pros and cons of which school to attend. Having you as a father is totally going to mess up my student aid. I'll have to start over. I want to go to law school. There's one at U of I."

Albert laughed. "Hey, I'm supposed to be the master negotiator here, not you. Besides, the University of Miami also has a law school and a much better football team."

"Okay, we have all summer to talk about that. Can I go back to Idaho?"

Albert nodded. "I might have you sell cars instead. You're good at talking people into stuff. Gwen tells me you don't have a cell phone. I'll have one for you when I get home tonight."

"Good morning, Dad." Gwen hugged Albert.

"Good morning, sweetheart." He handed her the letter. "It's official. You have a full-blooded brother."

"That's so cool." She hugged Austin.

"I'm off to work." He put his coffee cup in the sink. "Are you headed straight to the beach after breakfast?"

"No, we have to do some swimsuit shopping first. Apparently, these two don't have any."

"Oh." He creased his forehead. "Um, never mind. I don't want to know how you know that. Bye."

"Bye, Dad," they both said.

Ricardo strolled into the kitchen. Putting his hands on his hips he said, "You peeked."

"It wasn't like that. I turned my back when you got out of the pool. Dad put reflective tape on the windows to keep out the sun which I had forgotten about until you streaked across the patio and into your room. I tried not to look, really I did."

"Well, what did you think?"

"Nope, not going there. Let me get you guys some breakfast and then we'll go swimsuit shopping before we hit the beach."

"Oh, by the way, I forgot to tell you, Austin. My mom called last night. Lisa stopped by and told her to tell me to tell you that she loved you. We've got to get you a cell phone, Dude."

"Wow, she really said that? Wait, she was alone?"

"No, it was Lisa and three U.S. Marshals."

"U.S. Marshals?" Gwen spun around. "Who is this girl of yours? Why does she have U.S. Marshals around her?"

"Oh, I can explain that, just as soon as I know myself. I'm not allowed to ask her about them. Oh, and Lisa isn't her real name, but that's the only name I have to go on. Please don't tell your dad, I mean, our dad about that."

"You're calling Albert, Dad, now?" Ricardo asked.

"The paternity test came back. I'm bona fide."

"See, I knew we could find your father. I was right in making the call."

"Thanks for making that phone call against my wishes. Just never do something like that again."

Chapter Twenty-Two

The trip to the clothing store had been challenging. Gwen had insisted that they each get two or three swimsuits. Austin couldn't understand why he needed more than one. "I have at least six bikinis and three one-piece suits. You need more than one. If the one is still wet, you can wear the other one."

"Do you go swimming once a day?"

She smiled. "Sometimes more than that. I'll go by myself to the beach in the morning, then with friends in the afternoon, then take an afternoon swim in the pool. Get at least two suits. You're in Florida."

He sighed but picked out two. Ricardo had his two already and didn't object when Gwen bought them for Austin and him.

"I have my own money," Austin said.

"Yes, but I have Dad's charge card."

Austin smiled and gave her a thumbs up. "You win."

Austin stared out onto the ocean for the first time. He didn't even notice the hot sand at first. He couldn't see the far side. All the lakes he'd ever seen had a far side. He could never see from the top to the bottom of Lake Coeur d'Alene, but he could follow both shorelines down the side of the lake. Water enveloped the entire horizon here.

"Come closer," Gwen beckoned. "Aren't your feet hot? I have a beach towel over here closer to the water for you."

"Oh, you're right. My feet are hot." He scrambled over to the towel. "Thanks."

She handed him some sunblock and laid down on the blanket next to him. He began putting it on himself. "What are you doing?"

"You handed me some sunblock so I'm using it."

"For my back, silly."

"Oh." He spread it on her back. "Can I finish putting it on me?"

"Of course."

When he finished, he put the bottle back into her bag. "Thank you."

"Austin, look around. How many girls do you see?"

He scanned from side to side. "A lot."

"Dad says you're going back to be with a girl, but there are lots of girls here. Wait until you start at the University of Miami. You'll be amazed how many single girls there are."

"You'd be amazed that someone as good-looking as I am," he chuckled, "would have lots of girls hanging all over him. But the truth is, I've only had the one girlfriend and it was a recent thing. Also, Dad and I are still discussing where I go to school."

"Don't sell yourself short. I think you're adorable, and if I weren't your big sister, I might even be interested."

"Okay, if you had a choice between me, pretending I'm not your brother, and Ricardo, which one would you pick?"

"Hmm, I don't think you would win that one, little brother."

"See, there you go."

"I just figured out the problem." She sat up. "You've hung around Ricardo since grade school?"

"Yes."

"You need to hang around someone else. He's overshadowing you. Ricardo wasn't around when you met your girlfriend, was he?"

"Well, no. Now that you mention it."

Ricardo came running up, dripping water. "What are you two doing sitting here? The ocean's that way." He pointed. "Come on, let's have some fun."

All three ran towards the water, because of the hot sand. As soon as they were at the edge, they slowed down. Ricardo threw himself into the waves first, followed by Austin and Gwen.

They splashed around a while. Austin turned but didn't see the next wave. It knocked him off his feet and he rolled around the bottom for a minute, trying to stand up. A large hand grabbed his arm and pulled him to safety. "Watch the undertow." Ricardo let him go.

Austin made sure no more waves took him by surprise. His swimming shorts felt heavier. They had acted like a sand scoop when he had hit the bottom, but he ignored them. No way to fix that on a crowded beach.

"You look a bit uncomfortable," Gwen commented.

"I have sand in my swimsuit."

"I've done that, except bikini bottoms have a lot less room in them than your trunks. I swim out to the deep area where there's no one around and pull them down just far enough to get the sand out. Then I swim back, but mostly on days that I know the waves will be up, I wear a one-piece suit."

"Well, I can't do either one of those right now. The first one, you'll know what I'm up to, and the second one, they don't make those for guys."

"I guess you'll be grinning and bearing it."

"I guess."

Austin played in the waves some more. When he looked back, he saw Ricardo and Gwen, sitting on the towels next to each other, talking like they had been friends for years. *I wonder what they're talking about?* Then he realized he was the only thing those two had in common. *Ricardo's probably telling her all the embarrassing things I did growing up.*

Hours later, they headed home. Austin went to take a shower. A full cup of sand and small shells came out of his swimming shorts when he took them off. He felt guilty leaving it there because Ricardo would be taking a shower after him, so he cleaned it up. *No wonder I was so uncomfortable.*

After getting dressed, Austin walked out into the living room. Albert came home a few minutes later. "Here you go, Son. Your own cell phone. I bought you the latest and greatest. I know you don't know how to use it yet. I'll have Gwen teach you."

"Wow, thanks. I begged mom for even a flip phone, but there wasn't money in the budget for that. This is awesome."

"Here's the number. Memorize it because you'll be surprised how many people ask for it."

"Okay, great."

"I've already put my number in it."

Ricardo walked in a minute later. "Dude, you finally have a cell phone. Give me the number."

Albert smiled. "See what I mean?"

Chapter Twenty-Three

After breakfast, the next morning, Gwen drove them over to the car lot where her father worked. Albert came out to greet them when they arrived. He showed them the lot and then took them into the back office and introduced them to all the people. Most of the women hugged Austin. "Wow," they would say. "Albert's long-lost son."

Albert took Austin aside. "You'll inherit half of this when I'm gone."

"You're not dying anytime soon, are you?"

"No, I'm as healthy as an ox."

"Good. We don't have to worry about that anytime soon. I've lost my mom. I don't want to lose my newly found father."

"Is now a good time for you to pick out a car? I mean, if you decide to stay?"

"I don't even have a license. Besides, I want to see my girlfriend again. She's a goddess."

"Okay, but I don't do well with relationships. I hope this one goes better than mine did. You must really love her if you're giving up a car for her."

"I have a chance with this girl. I've got to see how it turns out."

"All right. You have a ticket. You fly out in a couple of days, but I'm going to send you clothes shopping with

Gwen anyway. I have furniture coming in the morning for your bedroom upstairs. It'll be all set up for when you come back home."

Home? Austin's heart skipped a beat. *I have a home.* He smiled. "Thanks, Dad. I so appreciate you." He hugged him.

Ricardo came in smiling. "Dude, Gwen's going to take us on a jet boat tour of the Everglades."

"Wow, that's cool. When do we go?"

"Tomorrow. Today she's taking you clothes shopping because you don't have enough, in her opinion, and then after getting you a learner's license she's going to teach you how to drive."

"Do I need more clothes, in your opinion?"

"All the clothes you own, except for what my mom bought you, should be thrown away. But, that's just my opinion."

Austin shrugged. "Okay then, clothes shopping it is."

They dropped Ricardo off at the house. He wanted to go swimming and not shopping. When they were finally alone, she said, "Dad says you're determined to go back to Idaho. I'm supposed to talk you out of it."

Austin shook his head. "I know I don't have much there, but I want the girl."

"Speaking by personal experience, I can tell you, first loves don't last. There are lots of girls here. I say you stay and give it a chance. Besides, the girl in Idaho must have some legal issues. It sounds like she's under house arrest.

That's a lot of security around her. I haven't told Dad about that, by the way."

"Thank you. Let's just do the clothes shopping. Ricardo thinks I should throw away most of what I own."

"I agree. We're going to buy a lot because we have to fill your dresser when it arrives later on today."

"Okay. All this is going to take getting used to."

"Don't worry about getting used to it. You're leaving, remember?"

He leaned back in the seat and didn't say a thing the rest of the trip to the mall. When they stepped into a store, Austin was appalled by the quantities of clothes she made him try on. Fifteen pair of pants lay in the basket when he came out with the sixteenth pair. "These fit, too. Which ones are we buying? I'll take the rest back."

She laughed. "You don't need to worry about taking anything back, we're buying all of these."

"I don't need sixteen pairs of pants. I usually only have one or two."

"These are formal, they will go nicely with the suitcoat we're about to buy you. These two are casual. You need at least two pair of each in case one is in the laundry. Everyone needs Levi's. I'm buying you four pair of those. These pants are resort casual so you can come with us to the Country Club. I'm going to have to teach you how to play golf. Oh, golf pants. We'll need two pair of those. Thanks for reminding me."

Austin sighed as she took him to sporting goods.

Back in the men's department, she had him try on shirts. He ended up with fourteen in the shopping cart.

"What do I need with fourteen shirts?"

She smiled. "I knew you were going to ask that. If we go on vacation, you'll need a shirt a day and since we usually go for two weeks, that's fourteen shirts, but we're not done with shirts yet. We need a couple of dress shirts for Dad's award ceremonies. We'll have to attend at least two a year. Then you'll need another couple of dress shirts for going out to dinner and church."

"Church?"

"Yes, every Sunday morning for an hour. You don't go to church?"

"No, Mom says it was too hard on the car driving to it once a week. I have gone a lot with Ricardo's family, though. I enjoyed it."

"Great. Now we need to talk about neckties. Can you tie one?" He shook his head. "No problem, I'll buy you a clip-on you can wear until Dad has time to teach you how to tie one. Then we'll get you three pair of shoes and underwear. I'll let you pick those out by yourself. And socks, of course."

When they were done, she brought out the charge card to pay the close to eight-hundred-dollar shopping bill.

Chapter Twenty-Four

"Okay, go a little slower. You took that last corner way too fast." Gwen's voice sounded strained.

"But I made it."

"That's not the point. You're supposed to be learning how to drive good, not bad. That's why Dad isn't teaching you how to do this. Now, turn at the next corner, slowly, and we'll try again."

After twenty times of driving around the neighborhood, Gwen deemed him ready to try a backroad. They drove down a country lane at forty-five. Gwen looked over to see Austin sweating and white-knuckling the steering wheel. "Can you turn on the radio?"

Looking down, trying to find the radio, the car swerved a little, so he looked back up. "No."

"Had enough for today?"

"Yes."

"Pull off up here and I'll take over." When they switched, she commented, "Not as easy as it looks, is it?"

"Thanks for everything, going with me to get the learner's permit and trying to teach me how to drive. I would like to practice a couple of more times before I leave."

"Sure, that's what big sisters are for." She leaned over and put an arm around him. "Let's see, I can go with you one more time, day after tomorrow for an hour or so. We don't have time tomorrow. Of course, if you don't leave, I can spend a lot of time teaching you."

He gave her a half-smile. "At least you don't give up easy."

"When Dad gives me an assignment, I give it my best shot."

"Why don't you come with me? Idaho is a wonderful state."

"I can't. I've taken too much time off work already. If I keep it up, Dad will realize he doesn't really need me at the lot."

Austin smiled. "Just a thought."

When they pulled up to the house, she sent Austin to get Ricardo while she took Austin's clothes upstairs to his new room. "Come check this out, guys," she called down the stairs.

As Austin entered his bedroom for the first time his eyes widened. "Wow, it's so large."

"It's bigger than my living room at home," Ricardo added.

"Your dresser is full of clothes and so now is your closet. It should feel right at home, I mean, it is your home now. You should stay."

"Has she been trying to talk you into staying all day long?" Ricardo asked.

"All day, today, and the whole time I've known her." Austin jumped on the bed. "It's so soft."

"And as soon as you move in here you can have this room and all the clothes that go with it. But since you've decided to go back, you'll have to stay in the guest room. Not Dad's rule, but mine."

"She's coming on hard, isn't she?"

"I'm right here, you know." She scowled at Ricardo.

"Your guest quarters are the nicest place I've ever stayed in. I'll be just fine down there."

"Suit yourself. I'm hungry and I don't feel like cooking. We're going out tonight. I'll have Dad meet us at the restaurant." She headed out the door.

The waiters looked right out of some of the black and white movies Austin had seen, including the napkin across the arm. He gasped as he opened the menu. "Sixty dollars for an entree?"

"This is Dad's favorite restaurant. We come here once a month or so. He has a good relationship with the owner. In fact, they buy all their cars from us and even their catering van. We are way ahead monetarily, so relax. Order anything you want. Don't worry about the price."

"Oh, sorry. I overreacted again, didn't I?"

She put her hand on his. "You will never have to worry about money again. I know it's a foreign concept to you right now, but you'll get used to it."

He nodded.

"Hi, my sweet daughter and my son. Hello, Ricardo. I got here as fast as I could. Did you order for me?"

"Not yet," Gwen replied. "The waiter hasn't made it to the table."

"Ah, Mr. Morgan." A smiling waiter said, "Do you want the usual?"

"No, I thought I'd try the bone-in ribeye today."

"Very good, and for you, Miss Gwen?"

"The usual."

"Very good, and who do we have here?"

"This is Ricardo. He's from Idaho."

"I'll have the same thing as Mr. Morgen."

"Very good, Ricardo. Now another new face."

"This is Austin, my son."

The waiter's eyes widened. "Your son?"

"Yes, I found my son after all these years."

"Oh, my. Carlos," the waiter ran off. "Carlos." Soon he came back with the owner. "Carlos, this is Austin, Mr. Morgan's long-lost son."

"Oh, wonderful." He hugged Austin from behind. "What a wondrous occasion. Today, your dinner is on me. Julian, bring them some wine."

The two left. "See, you worry too much about money," Gwen replied. "We won't even have to pay for this meal."

"That's great, only, I didn't get to order."

"Oh, no." When the waiter came back with the wine, she said, "You didn't take Austin's order."

"Carlos has ordered the tenderloin with lobster tail for you. If you don't like that, we will bring you something else."

"Oh, okay," Austin replied. He waited for the waiter to leave. "I've never heard of a tenderloin before. What type of animal is that?"

Gwen laughed. "It's a delicious part of a cow. Have you had lobster before?"

"No, but I hear it's good."

"Yes, very good," Ricardo replied.

When dinner came, Austin relished every bite. "Can I taste the wine?" he asked Albert.

"Just a little. You're underage. I don't want either of us to get into trouble."

He took a quick taste. "I don't like it."

"Good, that will save you a lot of money going forward."

"You did everything but lick your plate," Gwen says. "You must have liked it."

"I loved it."

"I've never seen you eat that much, and I've known you a long time," Ricardo said.

When the waiter came back by, he asked Austin if he was done.

Scanning his plate, Austin said, "Did I miss something? You don't eat the shell, do you?"

Julian smiled. "That was a silly question on my part. And for you, Madam, do you need a box?"

"Yes, I don't have quite the appetite as the men do."

"Stay here, I'll bring dessert."

Austin held up his hand. "I can't eat another bite."

"Carlos insists. I'll box that up, too."

Chapter Twenty-Five

Austin white-knuckled the armrests on the airboat. He hadn't been so scared since he tried to turn on the car radio while driving. The pilot of the boat didn't seem to care for anyone's safety as he headed deeper into the Everglades. He skimmed around islands going, what felt like to Austin, eighty miles an hour. Everyone in the boat sat upon elevated seats to enjoy the view better.

Finally, the boat slowed down as they gazed around. "Look to your left, that's an osprey in the tree there. If you look straight ahead, you'll see three pelicans flying along. I have an alligator friend around here somewhere. I call him Waldo because he's so hard to find, but one piece of chicken and he comes right out of his hiding place." The pilot threw a drumstick in the water and a large alligator swam up to the boat. Way too close for Austin's comfort. It swam back into the undergrowth after it grabbed the chicken leg. "Let's move on."

"This is a blast," Ricardo whispered to Austin. Gwen and Albert were in the seats behind them.

"If he'd slow down, it would be better."

"Nah, that's the fun part, little buddy."

Going slower this time, the pilot turned the corner then shut off his engine. "Below you are a group of manatees. They hang out here. We don't want to disturb them so we'll sit here until they move off."

One of the creatures stuck its nose above the water as if to see who was bothering them. Satisfied, he ducked back down. A few minutes later, he wandered off. The pilot started the boat again and drove it forward a few hundred yards. "Sometimes dolphins come into this channel. Keep your eyes open." They sat there for fifteen minutes, but no dolphins appeared. On the way back to the dock, the pilot pointed out interesting features, then he gunned it, leaving Austin to grab on again.

"That was a blast, thanks for taking us, Albert and Gwen," Ricardo said.

"Sure," Albert replied. "Tonight, you're in for a treat. I'm going to make you my meatloaf. It's a favorite of all."

Gwen nodded.

As Albert busied himself in the kitchen, Ricardo and Austin sat chatting in the living room when Gwen came in. "Am I interrupting?"

"No, in fact, we can use your advice. Should Austin bring Lisa flowers or not? I say he should, but he doesn't agree."

Austin shook his head. "My mom never had flowers and she survived."

"Your mom didn't have flowers because she couldn't afford them," Gwen said. "Flowers are a good thing. Don't bring her cheap flowers. Go to an actual florist."

"How much does a florist cost?"

"I would spend at least fifty on them."

"Fifty? I only have three hundred and fifty to my name."

She laughed, "You and money again. Dad's not going to send you there penniless. He even talked about putting you in an Airbnb, but when he asked Mrs. Fuimaono about it, she said she wanted you to stay with them for the summer. You're all set. He even sent her some money to help with groceries."

"Wow, she said that?" Austin replied.

"You know my mom loves you," Ricardo added. "You'd be so lonely by yourself."

"I just assumed I would be staying at your place. I'm glad your mom wants me to. I thought I was in the way."

"No, Dude. You're cool."

The meatloaf was the best that Austin had eaten. Of course, he didn't have much to compare it to, because his mom rarely made it and Ricardo's mom never made it during any of his visits.

That night Ricardo and Austin sneaked out the side door for a midnight swim only to find Gwen already there. "Come on in, guys, the water's fine." They both dove into the pool. She swam over to Ricardo. "I'm going to miss both of you, but you especially. You're such a hunk."

"Do I need to leave you two alone?" Austin asked.

"No," Ricardo replied. "What's gotten into you anyway?" he asked Gwen.

"I don't know. I keep thinking of the time, well, the other day. You know what I mean."

The door opened and Albert stepped out. "Oh, you're all here. I thought I'd take a quick dip before I went to bed."

Gwen backed away from Ricardo. "Come on in, Dad. We were just talking."

"You're really built, Ricardo. Do you work out?" Albert asked.

Before he could answer, Austin said, "Idaho first-string all-state football player. Timberwolves athlete of the year for two years in a row. He has five full-ride scholarship offers."

"Um, it's actually up to nine with a couple of more pending, but I think that I'm going to go to WSU so I can come home on the weekends."

"I'm going to tell Miami's coach about you. Would you even consider going here? We have a better record than WSU most years."

Ricardo gazed over at Gwen, she smiled and nodded her head. "I guess," he replied.

A half an hour later, when they had all left the pool, Ricardo knocked on Austin's door. "What was up with Gwen tonight?"

"I don't really know her that well, but maybe you should lock your door. Would you really consider coming here to Miami to go to school?"

"Not in a million years. I didn't want to hurt Gwen's feelings is all."

Austin nodded. "What do you think I should do?"

"If I, were you, I would go here. I'm going to WSU to be close to my family. You have that same chance to be close to your family."

"What about the goddess?"

"Who knows where she calls home? You don't even know her real name. At what point does she start living her life? Is there a trial she has to get through or is someone out to kill her just because they can? I don't know her story. Is she going to up and disappear one day?"

Austin shrugged.

"I'm going to bed, after I lock my door, that is. Good night."

"Good night."

Chapter Twenty-Six

Austin practiced his driving with Gwen. She seemed distracted, ignoring Austin for the most part. She finally asked, "Do you think Ricardo likes me?"

Austin pulled the car over to the side of the road. "He's dated every single girl in the senior class that agreed to go out with him. There are only a few who declined. He likes all women, but I haven't seen one that caught him yet. There is a junior from last year he talked about liking, but he's going away to college soon. He has nine scholarship offers so he'll end up somewhere. I'm thinking WSU. You may never see him again. I would give up on him."

"I guess you're right. Let's get back to driving. That last corner you took really sucked. You swerved too wide. Let's go out on the highway and see if you can turn the radio on while going fifty miles an hour."

"Okay."

When Albert had arrived home, Gwen had cooked hamburgers on the grill and had all the condiments out. "Looks good, let's eat." Over dinner, he turned towards Austin. "So, you're all packed up? Did all those new clothes fit in your suitcase?"

Gwen replied, "Those are Florida clothes. He can only have them if he stays here. He has his old clothes with him, except for the threadbare stuff. I threw those away."

"You went through my stuff?" Austin glared.

"Yes, big sisters are allowed to do that. I read that somewhere. I only threw away the disreputable stuff. Okay, it was about half, but you still have enough to last you until you come back home."

Austin sighed.

"Oh, I didn't know that was a thing," Albert replied. "See all the fun stuff I miss while I'm at work."

"You still have a chance, Austin." Gwen gave him a huge grin. "You can stay."

"I'm still going even if it means wearing a fig leaf home."

Ricardo choked on his laughter. "Don't do that. I'm sitting next to you, remember."

The rest of them laughed. After dinner, Austin checked his suitcase. Opening it up, he saw that some of his stuff had been taken out. He had to admit, he kept clothes longer than he should. All the clothes Ricardo's mom had purchased for him were there, but that was about it. He shut the lid. As he passed the hall he peaked out of the window and gazed out upon the pool. He didn't want to get his swimsuit wet and then put it back in the suitcase. *Wait, I have two and she didn't take those away. I can leave one here when I go.* Smiling, he donned his suit and jumped in.

A few minutes later, Ricardo and Gwen came out. "What are you doing?" Gwen asked.

"I had to take one more dip in the pool before I left. I have two swimsuits. I'll take one back home and leave this one here for when I come back."

She smiled. "So, you're planning on coming back. At least that's something. Wait here." Soon she came back down the stairs in her swimsuit and jumped into the pool also.

"I don't feel like changing and I'm not coming back, so I'll just sit here," Ricardo said.

Splashing around in the pool for an hour, Gwen and Austin raced back and forth, splashed each other, and saw who could hold their breath the longest. Finally, Gwen climbed out. "I'm going to bed. Dad will drive you to the airport. I'll see you when you get back, hopefully soon."

"Goodnight, Gwen," they both said.

Austin climbed out too. "It's late."

"Good night," Ricardo said as he stood up and went to his room.

In the morning, Albert had breakfast done when the boys staggered out of bed. He stuffed the suitcases in the car and drove them to the airport. When they arrived, he hugged Austin. "I know you're having a hard time letting go of your old life, but we love you. Come back soon." Shaking Ricardo's hand, he said, "Take care of my son. I don't want to lose him again."

"I will."

"Goodbye, boys."

When they finally sat down on the plane after checking their bags and getting through security, Austin turned to Ricardo. "Am I doing the right thing by leaving? Should I have stayed?"

"Dude, I would have stayed. He was going to give you a free car. There are lots of girls out there. Did you see how many were on the beach and a lot of them were our age?"

Austin slumped back down in his seat. "You and women. I asked the wrong person."

Ricardo elbowed him. "You gotta do what you gotta do."

"That's right." It wasn't long before Austin understood why Albert had upgraded them to first-class the last part of the previous flight. Ricardo's wide shoulders had Austin pinned to the side of the airplane. The window seat would have been nicer if he wasn't jammed up against the wall. "Can you lean the other way for a little bit?"

"Not without pushing the girl next to me into the aisle," Ricardo replied.

Austin sighed and went back to watching out the window. They landed in Denver so Austin went and stretched his legs. When the time came to board the next plane, he prepared for yet another uncomfortable flight. To his delight, no one sat next to Ricardo. "Scoot over and give me some room."

"Oh, yeah. Great idea."

They were both able to stretch out a little and when they arrived in Spokane, Austin had even been able to get some sleep on the plane. Ricardo's mom picked them up in front of the terminal.

"Did you have a nice flight?" she asked to no one in particular.

"Half of it," Austin responded.

Ricardo huffed, "I can't help the width of my shoulders. Albert complained about me on the way over and Austin's complaining about me on the way back." He stomped off.

"What was that all about?" Ricardo's mother asked.

"He's hard to sit next to. We had a seat between us on the last half of this flight and it was so much better."

"Oh, dear. I trust the rest of your trip went much better."

"Yes, I almost didn't come back."

Chapter Twenty-Seven

Austin stared out at the street from the front door. He wondered if he should have stayed in Florida. He didn't know what he should do next. *What if she changed her mind about me? What if she's moved? Is the reason she's there no longer valid?*

"Would you just go? You're letting the bugs in," Ricardo yelled.

Austin stepped out the door, shutting it behind him. *Well, here goes everything.*

Walking towards the private neighborhood, he wondered if one of the residents would notice him and kick him out. He passed the sign walked up to the house and knocked. Goose answered the door. "You're back."

"Is Lisa here?"

He didn't have to wait for an answer. She rushed to the door and threw her arms around him. "Austin. I was so worried. I thought you'd be tempted to stay in Florida and I'd never see you again."

"You know about Florida?"

"Nothing escapes the Marshals Service, Kid." Goose went back to his game as Lisa led Austin into the back bedroom.

"I have so much to show you. I found the great farmer's market that Goose has let me go to. They have these wonderful hand-thrown pots…" She looked up at the sound of squealing tires.

Goose rushed into the room and slammed the door behind him, as he tipped up the bed, the pots flew across the room and crashed into the floor.

"What's going on?" Austin asked.

Goose ducked behind the bed. Lisa pulled two guns out of her nightstand and handed one to Austin after she cocked it. "Don't hold it like that. The slide will come back and break your thumb. Put your thumb around the grip instead."

"How do you know so much about guns?"

"I come from a long line of criminals."

At the sound of splintering wood Goose open fired through the wall at the front door area. Lisa joined in. Those in the living room shot back. Plaster, wood, and lead came through the wall from both sides. After getting off several rounds, Austin felt something hit his shoulder. He clasped his one hand over it while he kept firing with the other.

"Stop shooting. That's my granddaughter in there." The guns went silent. "Sophia, honey. I'm here to talk you out of testifying against me."

"Grandpa, how did you get out of jail?" Lisa asked.

"I bought the judge. Honey, we're family. You don't want to do this."

"You're not a good person, Grandpa. How did you find me?"

"I know a guy in the FBI. Hey, that rhymes. I'm a poet." The men in the other room laughed.

"Boss." One of them said, "There are sirens coming this way. We got to go, there are only two ways out of this neighborhood."

"Sophia, I've got to go, but remember, a Russo doesn't testify against another Russo."

"But a Russo can have another Russo killed. How does that work, Grandpa?"

Tires squealed again as the car sped away. Austin set the gun on the ground. His head spun. *Don't faint, don't faint.*

"Austin, are you alright? You're bleeding. Goose, he's hit."

Everything went black.

Goose knew this call wasn't going to go well. He sat at the foot of Austin's hospital bed. Austin had just come out of surgery. The doctor said the bullet slowed down going through the wall and then through the bed. It could have been a lot worse. Dialing the number for 'Dad' on Austin's phone, he waited for an answer.

"Hello, Son. How's Idaho treating you?"

"Hello, Sir. This isn't Austin. I'm from the U.S. Marshals Service. I regret to inform you; your son's been shot."

"Shot, what do you mean shot!"

"If you'll let me finish, Sir. He's been hit in the shoulder. The doctors took the bullet out and he's expected to make a full recovery."

"Who shot him? Why did they shoot him? What's going on?"

Austin blinked twice then tried to sit up. A nurse pushed him back down. "Just relax. The doctor will be in to see you in a few minutes. You're not to move until then." She shook a finger at him.

He focused on someone at the foot of his bed. "Goose, what are you doing here?"

"I've been reassigned."

"Where's Lisa, Sophia, or whatever her name is?"

"I have no idea."

"But, Goose, I have to find her."

"We'll talk about this later."

The nurse ran back in. She glared at Goose. "His heart rate is up. Whatever you're doing, stop it."

"Yes, Ma'am."

She checked on Austin. "You need to relax. Take deep breaths and slowly exhale."

When he did so, she walked back out of the room.

"Okay, calmly, I have to tell my father what happened."

"I took care of that for you."

"Really, what did he say?"

"He didn't take it well. He threatened to sue me, the Marshal Service, the FBI, the U.S. Senate, and the President of the United States."

"What did you tell him?"

"Well, I told him you had been wounded. He wanted to know how. I told him you were involved in a shootout and were a real hero in defending my life. I didn't say anything about Lisa or whatever her name is now; pretty sure it isn't Lisa anymore. He asked why you were in a place where shootouts occur. I said you weren't. This was an entirely new thing for that area. He asked when did you learn to shoot a gun, and I said, in the middle of the firefight, but you picked it up real quick like. Oh, and I forgot to mention he's also threatening to sue the governor of Idaho and the mayor of Hayden."

"He sounds really upset."

"I know you were still sedated, but I'm sure you could hear him yelling anyway. Bottom line is, he's sending out your sister to pick you up. You're going back to Florida, and no, you don't have a choice this time."

"I pretty well had that figured." Austin sighed, he looked over at the monitors. "It's later."

"It's later than what?"

"You said we would talk about that girl whose name is no longer Lisa. How do I find her?"

"Ask the FBI, I guess. Sorry, interdepartmental row. Anyone who knew anything about her has been reassigned. The Marshal Service took all her information away from the FBI because they thought that was where the leak was. The FBI is furious and blaming the Marshal Service and especially you. I told them I was pretty sure it wasn't you. Why would you be in the middle of the firefight if you knew it was going to happen? They still don't have an answer for that one. Bottom line, she's gone, kid."

Chapter Twenty-Eight

Austin slept on and off during the night. Goose only left to get some food, otherwise, he sat or slept in the chair. With his medication wearing off, Austin had a hard time getting back to sleep. He couldn't believe how much his shoulder hurt. He watched Goose sit up and stretch. "Why do they call you Goose?"

"It's my name. My dad loved the movie Father Goose so much, he named me for it. Actually, he tried to name me Gosling, but my mother put the brakes on that idea."

"Aren't you going to work today? I mean, it's nice that you're here, but don't you have a job to do?"

He laughed. "After the fuss your father raised, I've been assigned to you until your sister gets here. I'm expecting her this evening around seven, so I don't have that much longer to go."

Ricardo appeared in the doorway. "Hey, Dude. Done any shooting lately?"

Goose reached into his jacket, but Austin held up his hand, "He's a friend."

"I recognize him now. I saw him at the graduation. Please, come in." Goose relaxed.

"I've done more shooting than I ever wanted to."

Mrs. Fuimaono slapped Ricardo on the arm. "You can't ask questions like that." Smiling at Austin, she said, "I brought you a treat. I hear hospital food is terrible." She set some PaniPopo down on the tray next to Austin's bed.

"Did you shoot one of the bad guys?" Ricardo asked.

"Ricardo," his mom glared at him.

"I don't know. I fainted before they did a body count."

Goose shook his head. "It didn't look like we got any one of those guys, but that wall will never be the same again."

Mrs. Fuimaono gave Goose a sideways glance.

"This is Goose. He was there during the shootout," Austin explained.

"Oh," Ricardo's mother replied. "I didn't read about any of this in the newspaper."

"You won't, either. We had the story squashed to protect those involved," Goose replied.

"You can do that?"

"Had to."

Turning her attention back to Austin, she asked, "How are you feeling?"

"The shoulder is hurting. They had me all numbed up when I came out of surgery, but now the meds are wearing off."

"I'll go get a nurse," she volunteered.

"You don't need to do that, I'll be okay."

She didn't listen. Soon a nurse entered the room. "I hear you're in quite a bit of pain."

"The numbness is wearing off," he commented.

"Let me see what the doctor put on your chart." After reading it, she walked out of the room. Coming back in with some pills and a cup of water, she said, "This will make you a little loopy."

He swallowed the pills down. "Thanks."

"We'll get out of your hair so you can get some rest." Mrs. Fuimaono pulled Ricardo out of the room.

"Bye," he said on the way out the door.

Sophia Russo stomped her foot. Her new handler had given her the name Karen and not by accident. "You have to at least find out how badly hurt he is." She wasn't getting any information on Austin.

"We will not call anywhere in Idaho from this location. Especially up to the Coeur d'Alene hospital. We don't want any traceability to here."

"Goose would have found out for me."

"Yes, good old Goose. Boy, am I tired of hearing about him. He didn't run a very tight ship, did he? Or maybe he's the leak."

"He isn't the leak. He saved my life. How could he be the leak?"

"That's still under investigation. He did let that kid over to visit you. Now there's nothing suspicious about him going from dirt poor to a fancy house in Florida."

"He found his father. Now, why would he turn on me? He got shot, remember?"

"That's a great way to divert attention from yourself."

"You're impossible. I'm going to pack my bags and go home. I'm done with this." She stomped down the hall.

He ran after her. "Wait. Let's talk about this. I'll find out how your boyfriend is, just don't leave."

Goose stood up. The nurse had come in with Austin's instructions and release papers. "I'll push the wheelchair. His sister is downstairs waiting for him."

"Okay," the nurse smiled. "Here you go." She ruffled Austin's hair. "Stay away from this guy. He's trouble."

He smiled up at Goose. "Don't I know it."

When they made it to the door, Gwen rushed up to him. "Austin, are you okay?" She went to hug him.

"Mind the shoulder."

"Oh, right." She hugged him off to the side. "What on earth happened?"

"That's classified, Ma'am," Goose replied.

She gave him a sideways glance.

"Gwen, this is Goose. Goose, this is my sister, Gwen."

"Oh, right. You're the one that got my brother shot. Dad says I'm supposed to slug you in the nose when I see you."

Goose held out his hands. "They were shooting at me, too."

"We have a red-eye back to Florida, but we've got to get moving or we'll miss the plane. I went over to Ricardo's house and gathered your things. Your bedroom in Florida is waiting. I even made the bed for you. Don't expect me to do that again." She looked at his sling. "Okay, maybe until you get the use of your arm back, but not after that."

"I can make my own bed."

"Anyway, I have an uber waiting. We've got to go." She glanced up at Goose. "Can you help get him in the car and I won't hit you?"

"It's a deal."

Chapter Twenty-Nine

Austin turned in his sleep, but the pain jolted him awake. "Ow."

"Are you okay? There's been a lot of moaning over there."

He sat up. "I can't stop hitting my shoulder." Even with the first-class seats, Albert bought for them, he kept turning onto his bad side. He gazed out the plane window. Lights shone from a small town. He didn't recognize anything in the darkness. "Will I ever see Idaho again?"

Gwen shrugged, but said, "Probably not. That girl of yours is trouble."

"She's no longer in Idaho."

"Where did she go?"

"Some secret location that they won't disclose. They moved her after the shootout."

Gwen stared at him for a second. "Wait, are you telling me the girl was in the room when the shootout occurred? No one mentioned her before."

"She's the one the bad guys were trying to kill. Her location was supposed to be secret, but someone gave her up."

"Okay, I've been super patient and not pressed the point about how you were shot. You and Goose were with the girl? Let's start from the beginning."

"I got my nerve up to go over that day…"

"No, I want you to start about how you met this girl and then get to the part where you're shooting at bad guys and getting shot."

He took a deep breath. "I was walking home when I passed this goddess sunbathing in her back yard. I guess I was staring when Goose came out back and threatened me. Goose is from the U.S. Marshals service and the girl, we'll call her Lisa, is in witness protection. Someone in the FBI leaked the information about her locations to the people she was testifying against." Austin shifted in his seat.

Gwen said, "Go on."

"Oh, anyway. She would hide and a tree when I passed by so Goose wouldn't see her talking to me. He found out anyway and told me to get lost again. Of course, I didn't. He finally began letting me in the house. Lisa and I were talking in her room when I heard the squealing of tires. Goose ran into the room and tipped over the bed. She had a couple of guns in the nightstand and handed me one. When Goose started shooting through the wall, I joined him."

"Wow." She sat back in her chair. "So, was it worth coming back?"

"Yes, and no. Yes, because I know she likes me a lot and no, because now I've lost her."

"She and Goose are still alive because of you. The extra firepower probably saved them."

A tear rolled down his cheek. "That's the first time I've said it out loud."

She turned. "Said what out loud?"

"I've lost her." She leaned over to put her arm around him. "Watch the shoulder."

"I know, I know." She rubbed his arm. "We'll find your mystery girl somehow. Maybe we'll wait until after the trial. That way, she won't be such a hot target."

"Hopefully." He snuggled down in his seat and tried to sleep some more.

They landed mid-morning. Albert waited in baggage claim for them. "Austin." He put his arm around his son, being careful not to touch the shoulder. "Come, I'll take you home. Someday, I want to hear all about it."

Austin had expected him to fuss about going back to Idaho and getting hurt. All he saw from Albert was the look of a concerned parent. "Thank you. I would love a hot shower and a bed. I need to catch up on all the sleep I didn't get last night."

"Be careful not to get your bandage wet," Gwen replied.

Albert turned to Gwen. "That was a quick trip for you. How are you holding up?"

"I'm good. I have Austin's pain pill prescription from the hospital. We can go pick that up after we get him to bed."

"Okay, sounds good."

They dropped Austin off at the house and headed out. He looked down at the key to the house, his key to his large house in Florida, then over at his bandaged arm. His life had completely changed since he saw the girl sunbathing in the backyard. Opening the door, he went upstairs to his room. He could see Gwen's touches in the decorating. She painted the walls light green and had pictures of seashells and ocean scenes on the walls. In the corner sat his very own computer. He didn't know where the doors in the room led to. The first one he opened had a walk-in closet with more clothes than he remembered buying. *She must have gone back out and done more shopping now that she knew my sizes.*

The other door led to a bathroom with a shower. *I have my very own bathroom, wow.* Taking a quick shower, he went through his drawers to find where she had put his pajamas and underwear. Getting dressed, he slipped into bed. He fell asleep as soon as his head hit the pillow.

Gwen turned to her dad when they left the driveway. "We need to talk."

"What's wrong, Honey?"

"It's Austin. He's lost his mother. He's moved all the way across the country. He's hurting. It's not only his arm, but it's his girlfriend, too. She's gone and he has no way of finding her. He doesn't even know her real name. He needs us more now than ever. Can you take a few days off work so we can spend time with him?"

"Okay, yes." As he drove his eyes suddenly widened. "You said he doesn't even know her name?"

"No. She's in witness protection. That's why she had security around her. The bad guys found where she was located and they tried to take her out. Austin, Goose, and the girl retreated into the back bedroom and drove them off.

148

When the shooting was over, they took him to the hospital and hid her in another town."

"Wow, that's a crazy story. So, Austin was the only one shot?"

"Yes, according to Goose."

"You met Goose? Did you punch him in the nose like I told you to?"

"No, of course not. He took care of Austin at the hospital. He even rolled him down to me when I pulled up at the door then helped him into the car. I couldn't very well hit him after he did all that."

He sighed. "I suppose not."

They arrived back before Austin woke from his nap. Gwen lay on the couch for twenty minutes. When Austin did wake up, he headed towards the computer. *Is this thing on the internet?* He opened a web browser. "Yes."

He typed in Sophia Russo. He had heard both names that fateful day. The grandfather had called her Sophia, and he had also said, "A Russo doesn't testify against another Russo."

To his amazement, a lot of articles popped up. "Russo Family Crime Lord has been Arrested on Murder and Racketeering Charges."

"Sophia Russo is Set to Testify Against Her Grandfather."

"Heir Apparent to the Russo Crime Family, Tony Russo, Gunned Down in the Streets."

One, in particular, caught his interest. "Louie Russo Back in Jail after a Shootout with Federal Agents. Teenage Bystander Shot, but he is Expected to Survive."

Bystander? I was a participant. He read further down. "At an undisclosed location." *They wouldn't have known where Hayden is anyway.*

He read everything he could find, but he couldn't figure out when the trial was. *Do I dare show up even if I know?* His heart raced. Reasons for saying yes and saying no went through his mind.

Chapter Thirty

"Hi, Dad." Austin gave him a sideways glance. "I thought you'd be at work."

"No, I've decided to spend some time with my son and daughter. How would you like to go to Little Havana and pick up some food for dinner? Then we'll go introduce you to your grandmother. She's been dying to meet you. She was out of town the last time you were here."

"Sounds great. I was hoping you picked up my prescription. My shoulder is killing me."

"Yes, it's right here." Gwen held up the bottle. "They only gave me two days' worth because it's powerful stuff and you're supposed to take it with food. I'll make you a quick sandwich."

"Don't do that. I know where the kitchen is. I live here now."

She smiled. "That's so good to hear you say that, but I'm still making you my signature sandwich. Sit down at the table and I'll be right back."

A few minutes later she came out with a glass of milk, two pills, and a large sandwich on a Kaiser roll. "I hope you don't have any food allergies."

"Why, what's in it?"

"Pretty much everything." He picked it up and gazed at it. "Don't look, eat."

He took a large bite. "Mmm. Let me guess, bacon, lettuce, tomato, some type of lunch meat, pickles, mayonnaise, and something else I can't identify."

"Good. There are two types of lunch meat, chicken breast, and salami. Also, provolone cheese, salt, pepper, and a hint of tabasco."

"Well, if I die of a food allergy today, at least I will die happy." He took another bite. He then swallowed his pills, chased down with a gulp of milk. He finished his sandwich and said, "What's Little Havana?"

"It's a part of Miami the refugees from Cuba settled in. Of course, it's now a mix of cultures. You'll love it. Come on." Albert stood up and headed for the door. Austin followed. Soon the three of them were driving through town.

Austin watched out the window, seeing a lot of brightly colored buildings, mostly yellow, but some red and an occasional green one. The skyscrapers of Miami stood in the distance. The car stopped at a meat market in a strip mall and they went in. Albert picked up eight steaks.

"Let me get this straight," Austin smiled. "You're buying Australian and Japanese steaks in a Cuban meat market."

"Yes."

"Isn't that going to cause an international incident somewhere?"

"Just wait until you taste it." Gwen patted him on his good shoulder. "It's great. Granny has this amazing grill in her backyard. Dad loves cooking steaks on it."

They drove down the street and stopped in front of an orange building. Going in, Albert picked out all sorts of produce. "This is going to be great, little brother." Gwen passed him and put some zucchini in the basket.

"Don't be shy." Albert urged, "if you see something you like, get it."

Austin put cucumbers in the basket. He then picked up an Anaheim pepper. "What's this?"

"Oh, those are good." Gwen took it from him and put it in the basket.

"Okay." Austin shrugged. He didn't dare ask another question as he didn't know what he would end up with. He walked the aisles looking at a lot of unfamiliar produce.

Gwen called out from the check stand, "We're ready to go. Granny called. She's so excited to see you."

He followed them out the door. They drove across town to a nice neighborhood. His grandmother's house sat back from the main road. The houses around it were brown and beige, a far cry from the colorful ones in Little Havana.

"This is it. Let me introduce you to Granny. Oh, don't call her that. She hates it. Call her Bee or Grandma Bee."

"Thanks for the heads up." Austin waited on the front porch until a woman with curly grey hair answered the door.

"Austin, is this really you? We've been looking for you for years." She opened the door and went to throw her arms around him.

"Watch the shoulder." He stepped back.

"Oh, are you hurt?" She turned to Albert. "How did he get hurt?"

"Old football injury. It's acting up on him again," Albert replied.

Austin sputtered, but Gwen stepped on his foot. "Ow."

"Shh," Gwen whispered. "Grandma Bee, we brought steaks."

"Oh, good. Where are my manners? Come in." She led them through the overly stuffed house.

A small lane through the living room was all they had. Furniture and rugs, with lots of pictures on the walls, were the décor. Austin stopped to look at one of the photos. His mom and Albert were both smiling. She had on a wedding dress and he had on a tux.

"I don't know why she keeps that one," Albert whispered to him on the way past.

"She's beautiful."

"Yes. That was a great day. Things fell apart from there." Albert headed out the back.

Gwen came up and looked over his shoulder. "One of these days I'll have you sit down and tell me all about her."

"I would love that. By the way, it's not an old football injury. I was shot," he whispered back.

"If you tell her that, she'll die of a heart attack right in front of you. If you don't want her to do that, well, go with the football story. I would have come up with a better story than that, but dads not good at spare of the moment. We should have planned out what to say a little better."

"I hope she isn't a football fan because if she starts asking me questions about the game, I'm going to be at a loss. I've never even seen a game. What Ricardo told me about the sport is all I know."

"No worries. I'll run interference for you."

"Thanks."

Chapter Thirty-One

It looked like a feast to Austin. Steaks, grilled zucchini, stuffed peppers, a tossed salad, and lemonade to drink. He sat down next to Gwen.

"What type of salad dressing would you like, Austin?" his grandmother asked.

"Oh, just Italian."

"When you injured your shoulder, what position were you playing?"

Gwen pipped up. "He's a receiver, all though, with his injury he might not play again."

"Oh, dear. What happened?"

"He was going for the ball when this great big burly lineman smashed into him," Gwen replied.

"Poor thing." She turned to Albert. "I heard you found a good lineman for the Hurricanes. What happened there?"

"It looks like he's headed to Washington State. He wants to be able to go home on weekends."

She turned back to Austin who had just taken a forkful of steak. "Where are you planning on going to school?"

He swallowed. "It looks like I'm going to the University of Miami. Dad doesn't want to let me out of his sight since I was, um." He could feel both Albert and Gwen glaring at him. "Since my, um, football injury."

Gwen winked at him from behind Grandma's back. "You could walk on to the team in the fall then. They are always looking for receivers. I'll introduce you to the coach."

"Grandma, he's done with football because of his shoulder. It makes him sad to talk about it."

"Well, that's too bad. You can go to the games with me. I have season tickets."

He scowled at Gwen, then gave his grandmother a feeble smile. "Okay, great."

"These fried zucchinis are wonderful, Dad. You have just the right amount of seasoning on them."

"Thank you, I'm trying a different recipe."

Glad they had changed the subject, Austin wished they hadn't done it so blatantly. Austin had just met her, but he couldn't help but think she knew more about what was going on than they realized. Taking another bite of beef, he barely had to chew it. It nearly melted in his mouth. He had seen how much Albert had spent on it. *I know, don't worry about money, but I do.* He couldn't get in that mindset that Gwen kept preaching. Still, the steak was amazing.

"So, tell me, Austin. Do you have a girl back in Idaho?"

Gwen nearly spit out her drink. "Excuse me," she said. "I swallowed wrong."

"She moved suddenly, but I think she still likes me."

"Where did she move to? Somewhere closer to Florida, I hope."

"She could be right next door, for all I know. She needs to do some things before she'll contact me again. I'll sit and wait and hope. I didn't really tell her where I moved to either. We'll see."

"I know long-distance relationships are hard, but I bet it's a lot harder when you don't know where they are."

"Grandma, it's a sore subject with Austin right now," Gwen interjected. "Can we talk about something else? How's your bridge club going?"

As they talked about the different personalities of the bridge club, Austin's thoughts wandered back to Lisa. *Sophia Russo. I found her real name. Now if I can only find her.*

"What do you think, Austin?" Grandma asked.

He looked up from his stupor. "I'm sorry, I wasn't paying attention."

"Thinking about the girl, I bet. I'm so sorry I brought her up. Anyway, I was asking about playing cards with someone who sneezes a lot. Some have said we should ban him from the club because of it."

"He just has allergies. Get him a box of tissues."

Grandma laughed. "Why didn't I think of that? I'll bring a box of tissues to our next club night. That'll end the problem. You're such a smart boy."

Austin watched as Gwen rolled her eyes out of Grandma's view. "Thank you," he muttered.

After dinner, on the way home Gwen commented, "You're such a smart boy. She never says that to me."

"You're not a boy."

"You know what I mean. Bring some tissues, you're such a smart boy."

Austin shrugged. "I can't very well help what she says, now can I. Oh, by the way, thanks for covering for me with that football thing."

She folded her arms and leaned back in her seat. "Welcome."

"Now, Gwen. Don't be that way," Albert replied. "You know your grandmother's just trying to involve Austin. She's being overly nice because he's new to the family."

She sighed. "I suppose you're right. It's just that I don't feel she notices me. When we go over she talks almost exclusively to you and now that Austin is here, she's talking to him. Does she not see that I'm in the room?"

"She's always been partial to men, you know that. Don't let it get to you."

"It does sometimes."

Austin cleared his throat. "Does anyone in my mom's family still live around here?"

An awkward silence ensued for a few minutes; finally, Gwen said, "They are not nice people. I tried to connect with them for a while, but in the end, they ran me off. Besides, I think our grandfather is in jail the last I heard. He has a bit of a drinking habit and he supplements his income by selling drugs. I think that's why they didn't want me around, because all sorts of strange people come to their house all hours of the day and night."

"Oh, I see. Not someone I'd want to hang around with."

"Probably not," Albert added.

Chapter Thirty-Two

Gwen had put off driver's training until Austin's arm healed. Then they started back in on it. He could finally turn on and off the radio and even change stations, without driving them into a ditch.

The day came when he received his driver's license. He did everything perfectly except parallel park. Gwen couldn't do it so she didn't teach Austin how to. Still, he had given it his best effort.

Afterward, he went to drive Gwen home, she stopped him. "Oh, no, you don't. This is my car and I'll drive it. I'm taking you to see Dad at work."

"Oh, okay."

When they arrived there, Albert came out of the office. "Well, congratulations, Austin. Pick out a car."

"Wow, really?"

"Not a new one, though. Stick to the used ones."

"Oh, okay. Awesome." Austin drove several cars including a red sports car. He could see Albert cringing when he took it out. *He's either worried about me or worried about how much this one costs.* Austin decided not to pick that one. He settled on a sensible four-door car, not unlike the one his mother used to drive, except a decade newer. When he came back to the lot, he announced, "This is the one."

Albert smiled, but Gwen said, "A sedan, really? I thought for a minute there you were going to go for the

Mustang. It's the souped-up one. Zero to sixty in four and a half seconds. I'd been driving that if it had been on the lot when I came to get a car."

"It has a lousy back seat," Austin replied.

She folded her arms. "Exactly what are you planning on doing in the back seat?"

Austin blushed. He hadn't realized how that sounded until she said something. Albert took the keys, "Never mind about that. I'll get my finance guy to do the paperwork. You'll be all set in a few minutes. Meanwhile, look around. You start work on Monday. I'm going to put you in the sales department starting out. We are down several salesmen. Gwen, you, too. I'll have you show him the ropes."

She gave him the thumbs up. "Okay, Dad. I'll have to teach him about cars too, especially that the Mustang is a much more desirable car than a sedan."

"If you love Mustangs so much, why don't you trade in your car and get it?" Austin asked.

"How about it, Dad?"

"No, you drive crazy enough already. I don't want to give you an opportunity to drive crazy and fast."

She frowned, then turned to Austin, "Race you home." She didn't wait for a reply.

"She forgot about the paperwork," Albert said. "She'll think you're lost. I'll let her stew and then call her. Meanwhile, have a seat. It'll only take a minute."

When he had all the paperwork taken care of, Austin sat down in his car. Adjusting all the mirrors twice or three times, he pulled out carefully. He drove home taking the back roads. He had never driven home before, but Gwen had shown him how to use the GPS on his phone so he wasn't worried.

Gwen's car sat in the driveway, so he parked next to her. He knew his dad always parked in the garage, so he made sure to leave him enough room to get by. Walking up to the house, Gwen opened the door. "Did you get lost?"

"No, I had to do the paperwork, remember?"

"Nope, I didn't remember that. Go get your swimsuit on. We're going to the beach. Since our summer of fun will only last until the weekend, we'll make the most of it. I'll drive."

"Okay, but don't look at my scar. It's ugly."

"Oh, don't be self-conscious. It'll be okay."

He changed into his swimsuit but put a t-shirt on. He came running out a few minutes later. As they drove towards the beach, she said. "I invited a couple of my friends. I hope you don't mind."

He shrugged. "Okay by me."

When she stopped the car in front of a tan house, two girls came running out.

"See, if you would have had the Mustang, they wouldn't have fit," Austin commented.

"If I had the Mustang, we would have taken your car."

When they sat down, one of them said, "I'm Cindy. You must be Austin. I've heard so much about you."

"I'm Laura. Is it true you got shot?"

"Hi," he replied. "Yes, but it's mostly healed now."

"Oh, can we see the scar?" Cindy asked.

"Maybe when we get to the beach." Austin scowled at Gwen.

"You're famous. I've told all my friends about you. Maybe we can get you a girlfriend before the end of summer."

"I have a girlfriend."

"I mean get you a girlfriend who's safe to be around. The one you have, got you shot."

He sank down in the seat and sighed. He suddenly didn't feel like going to the beach. *Is this show and tell? Here's my brother who was shot and this is his scar. I stopped doing that in kindergarten.*

When they arrived at the beach, Austin walked out into the sand and put down his beach towel. Sitting down, he noticed Laura and Cindy sitting down next to him. "Well," Cindy said. "Show us your scar."

Reluctantly, Austin took off his shirt. Laura didn't look, but Carol ran her finger across it. "Did it hurt?"

"It still hurts, so, please be careful."

She snuggled closer. "You poor thing. I'll kiss you to make it better."

To his surprise, she kissed him on the lips, not on the shoulder. "I, er, I'm going in the water." He headed towards the ocean.

Cindy followed. "Wait for me."

He splashed around for an hour with Cindy right next to him the whole time. Laura and Gwen joined them after a while too. Austin kept trying to keep Gwen between him and Cindy, but he failed.

He went back up the beach to dry off.

Cindy threw her arm around him. "That was so much fun. We'll have to do this again sometime."

Chapter Thirty-Three

After they dropped Cindy and Laura off, Austin turned to Gwen. "What's going on with Cindy? She was all over me like glaze on a donut."

"I was as surprised as you were. I had forgotten what a gold digger she was."

He creased his brow. "What's a gold digger?"

"A girl that's after you for your money."

He shrugged. "I don't have any money."

"Oh, yes, you do. Dad has something to tell you when you get home."

"Can't you just tell me?"

"It's not my story to tell."

"So now I have to worry about if the girl likes me for me, or they want me for some money I might have, but I don't know about."

"Exactly."

"That makes me want to stick with the girl I had before any of this happened to me."

"Yes, but you don't even know where she is."

Austin sat there for a second wondering if he should tell his sister or not. She had accepted him without reservation so he decided to tell her. "I found her."

"What? I thought you didn't even know her name."

"During the shootout, her grandfather called her Sophia and then said a Russo didn't testify against a Russo."

"Sophia Russo? Wow, where is she?"

"I don't know where she is right now, but in a month, she'll be at the trial. She's testifying against her grandfather."

"You're not going, are you? They tried to kill you last time."

"They didn't know I was there. I was collateral damage. They were after her, not me."

"I don't know if Dad will agree to you going, but if you go, I want to go with you."

He smiled at her. "Thanks. I'll think about it. Let's not tell him about this quite yet."

"Okay. I don't like keeping secrets from Dad, unless, of course, they're my secrets, but I can do this for you. Are you going to tell him last minute?"

"I was thinking of waiting until I was already on the road."

She nodded. "I like the way you think. I worried about you when I first met you. You looked like a lost sheep, but I see now, you're going to do just fine."

"Thanks."

When they arrived home, Albert stood in the backyard at the grill cooking hamburgers. When they walked out, he said, "Beach day, huh?"

"Yes, we took Carol and Laura with us. Carol made a pass at Austin, but he fumbled."

"More like didn't try to catch the ball," Austin replied. He took his shirt off and jumped into the pool.

"Great idea," Gwen replied and jumped in too.

"Guys," Albert said. "How would you like to go deep-sea fishing on a charter tomorrow?"

"I'm in," Gwen replied.

"Do we have to eat them if we catch them?" Austin asked.

"The way Dad cooks the fish we catch, you'll love them."

"I'm in, too, I guess."

"Great, after dinner I'll make some calls. Did you want me to invite Carol, too?"

"Yes," Gwen answered, but then she giggled.

"No," Austin replied.

When Albert had dinner on the picnic table the two of them jumped out of the pool. Not bothering getting dressed, they sat down.

"Dad, can you explain why Carol is so interested in Austin?"

"Because he's a good-looking guy like his father."

"Well, that, too, but he doesn't think he has a dime to his name."

"I have three-hundred and fifty still," Austin interjected.

Albert snorted. "You have a lot more than that. Your grandfather left Grandma Bee half of his money when he died. He split the rest of it between the three of us. I got half of what was left and you two were given a quarter of the rest."

"Tell him how much money that was," Gwen coaxed.

"Your share, Austin, was over half a million."

Austin sputtered, "What?"

"See, I told you not to worry about money." Gwen nudged him.

"I didn't even think he knew I existed."

"He did. You were born before your mother took off and disappeared. She did mail a card from Wyoming saying you were safe. Your grandfather hired a private detective to find her, but it turns out, he was looking in the wrong state. Your grandparents on the other side fed her a little money, I think, because she never had a job. She wasn't on any government assistance. She didn't have a driver's license. She simply didn't exist, paperwork-wise."

Austin sat back in his chair. "This is all so hard to take in."

Albert continued. "I've also contributed to your account over the years. If I gave Gwen money, I put the same amount in the bank for you. I hoped to see you one day and wanted to be fair."

Gwen smiled. "So how much is in there now?"

"The app is on your phone, Austin. Here, I'll show you how to find it." Austin grabbed his phone from his pants and handed it over to Albert. "Your user ID is 'missingson' and your password is the car lot's name." He handed the phone back.

Austin's mouth dropped open. "Seven hundred and ninety-five thousand!"

"You also have about eighty thousand in your other account, but some of that will go for tuition. You've been accepted to Miami, by the way."

Gwen shook her head. "You were accepted before Dad applied for you. Grandma Bee is a huge donor to the school. They didn't know what your GPA was even. They were really pleased to see you had a three-point nine-five. I thought my grades were good, but I don't hold a candle to you."

"You applied for pre-law. I hope that's all right," Albert asked.

Austin still stared down at the number on his phone. "Um, yes, great."

Chapter Thirty-Four

The waves pitched the boat up and down. Gwen stared at Austin until he would turn her way, and then she would pretend she wasn't looking. Finally, he said, "What?"

"Oh, I just wanted to see if you were getting seasick."

"I guess not. I haven't thought about it at all."

"Good. I talked a date into taking me out here. He would get sick, take a seasick pill, crash for twenty minutes, then get up and get sick again. He was either sick or sleeping the whole time. He wasn't a whole bunch of fun. Then for some reason, he wouldn't go out with me after that. I think he was embarrassed over the whole thing."

"Sounds like."

Albert set his hook and began reeling in. When the fish came up against the boat a deckhand grabbed the net and pulled it in. "Wow, Dad, a yellow tail."

Austin walked over to see the silvery-sided fish with yellow highlights. "That's such a beautiful fish." A minute later his eyes went wide. "Wait, we're not going to eat that, are we?"

"Oh, yes, we are. It's so good," Gwen answered.

"Poor fish," Austin muttered.

"Don't get attached to the fish. They're dinner, not dinner guests," Albert replied.

Austin felt something tug on his line. In half a second, Gwen stood at his shoulder. "Set the hook. Pull up on the pole. Keep the line taut, don't let it go slack or the fish will spit out the hook. Reel in when the fish isn't running the other way. That's it, let the fish take some line out so you don't break it. Reel now. Okay, great job." The deckhand netted the fish. "Another yellow tail."

Austin gazed down at the fish. "Sorry."

"Will you stop it? It's…" Gwen's poled jerked so she didn't finish her thought. She reeled and tugged at the fish until she had it in the boat. "There, one each. Dinner's going to be wonderful."

They caught a few other types of fish like red snapper and some bottom fish. At the end of the day, the yellow tail seemed to excite Gwen and Albert the most.

By the time the boat tied up at the dock, the deckhand had filleted all the fish and put each in its own bag. When he handed Austin his fish, Austin held it up. "I'm so sorry. Here you were swimming around happily just looking for something to eat and I tricked you and dragged you out of your environment, then they cut you up."

"That's it." Gwen said, "We're cooking yours first so you won't have to think about it anymore. It's lucky for us we don't raise beef. You'd never be able to eat a hamburger again."

Austin heard Albert laughing in the background. Austin gave his bag to Gwen. "I guess I'm okay with cooking it. It's kinda too late to throw it back."

Albert lit the grill as soon as they arrived home. Gwen stood in the kitchen making the sauce while Albert fried the fish. When he deemed they were perfectly cooked, he slid them on a platter and took them inside for Gwen to put the magic on them.

With green beans and rolls to round out the meal, they sat down to eat. "Which one's mine?" Austin asked.

"I mixed them all up so you wouldn't get sentimental," Albert replied.

Austin took a forkful. "Say, this is good."

Gwen and Albert smiled at each other. "I told you Dad knows how to cook them."

"Oh, and you did great with the sauce."

Austin took another bite, then downed a roll. "I had fun today. Thanks for taking me."

"I'm glad. Are you excited to start work on Monday?"

"More apprehensive. I've never tried to sell anything to anyone. I've never had anything to sell that anyone else would want, I guess."

Gwen patted his hand. "Don't worry, I'll be there every step of the way to help you out.

"Great." He smiled. *Does she realize I know nothing about cars?*

That night he stared up at the ceiling. He couldn't sleep with his mind racing. *What would Mom think of me now? Would she think I have gone over to her enemy?* A chill went up his spine. *Her enemy? How selfish she was to keep me from them. Why didn't she want to try to visit her daughter, her own flesh and blood? What type of person was she that the judge wouldn't let her have custody of Gwen? What happened? Can I really be thinking these things about my mother?* He shook himself awake and headed downstairs to get a snack. To his surprise, Albert sat there sipping his coffee while reading the paper.

"Good morning, Austin. You're up bright and early."

"Is it morning? I thought it was the middle of the night."

"No, it's seven in the morning. I can cook you something to eat if you want."

"No, how about I cook you breakfast. How do you like your eggs?"

"Over medium, thanks."

Austin cooked eggs, bacon, hashbrowns, and then poured two glasses of milk. "I didn't sleep a wink last night. I'm going to need a nap sometime today, but now that I have you here, I want to ask some questions about my mother."

"I knew this day would come," Albert took a sip of his milk. "I wasn't looking forward to it."

"Sorry," but Austin went on anyway. "What attracted her to you?"

"Are you kidding, she was gorgeous. She was so much fun to be around. We would go out and have a good time."

"So, what happened?"

"The problem there was, she continued to have fun even after we were married. She was a party girl who thought I worked too much so she partied without me. She would be gone all hours of the day and night, spending my money along the way. Getting pregnant with Gwen slowed her down. I thought that we would be a normal family, but then when Gwen turned one, your mother began the party life again. I couldn't take it so I filed for divorce. With the threat of having her money cut off, she settled down again. For a year we were a normal family, I thought. She would leave two-year-old Gwen home alone while she went out, then sneak back home before I came home from work. I found out about it when she was arrested on drug charges."

"Oh, no. She wasn't like that when I knew her. Is that why the judge granted you full custody of Gwen?"

"Yes, with only supervised visits for her, but she never visited. When I found out she was pregnant, I went back to court to get custody of you. Since you weren't born yet, they wouldn't grant it to me. I fought that battle until you were one. The state did a welfare check on you and found you were living in squalor. I took her back to court. When I won, she took you and fled."

"I had no idea. Why do you suppose she never tried to contact Gwen?"

"It's simple. If she would have surfaced, we would have taken you and arrested her for kidnapping."

A wide-eyed Austin sat back in his chair. "I was a victim of kidnapping? I never realized that."

"That woman hid well. She didn't dare contact anyone from her past life except for her parents and those two are criminals to the core, so they wouldn't ever give her up. I think they were funneling money to her somehow. I don't know, but I suspect."

Chapter Thirty-Five

"I smell bacon," Gwen walked into the kitchen in her bathrobe. "Austin, you look like you've seen a ghost."

"I just realized that my less than idyllic life growing up was less idyllic than I thought it was."

"What does that even mean?"

"I asked too many questions about my mother. I've always said, if you don't want the answer, don't ask the questions, but I went and asked them anyway, and guess what? I didn't like the answers." He turned back to Albert. "That's why she was always so frail. She ruined her health early on by partying constantly."

"Let's try this again," Gwen said. "I smell bacon."

"Let me cook you up something. How do you like your eggs?" Austin headed towards the stove.

"Oh, it's *you* cooking. I like sunny-side up."

"I can't do sunny side up, how about over medium?"

"Dad doesn't do sunny side up either. Over medium will be fine." She grabbed a plate and a glass of orange juice. "I didn't know you could cook."

"Mom was sick most of my life. Somedays it was cook or starve."

"Oh. I don't remember her much, just hazy ideas of what she was like."

Austin quieted down. Lost in his own thoughts, he cooked the eggs, bacon, bagel, and hash browns and set them in front of Gwen. "Here you go."

As she ate, Albert asks, "Do you go to church, Austin?"

"Um, not really. I think Mom took me to church once or twice, but it just wasn't important to her."

"We have a lot of friends from our church who want to meet you. I was wondering if you would come with us today, so I can show you off."

He shrugged. "Sure."

The chapel sat on a corner lot, just a few blocks from the ocean. It looked like one of the old Spanish missions Austin had read about. Two towers protruded up the main building with one covered in ivy. A massive door opened to let the congregation in. Red carpet ran down the middle of the chapel with pews on either side. The inside seemed small to Austin. He had expected it to be larger to match the largeness of the outside.

As the family walked up the aisle, other parishioners nodded and smiled at them. Sitting three rows up from the front they settle in.

The preacher, dressed in a robe, greeted the congregation. Then the choir came out and sang. *Wow, they're good*, Austin thought.

The preacher quoted the Bible as he beckoned all to come unto Christ. When he finished, the choir came out and sang one more song, then the assembly ushered out and a crowd formed on the front lawn. Austin hadn't made it two steps before a girl threw her arms around him. *Cindy. H*e sighed.

A middle-aged woman approached. "So, this is the boy you were telling me about. Hi, I'm Cindy's mom. She's told me so much about you. I'm so glad you're out of the wild west."

Austin tried to sidestep Cindy, but it only made her grip tighter. "Isn't he adorable? And when we went to the beach the other day, he showed me his scar."

"Wow, I want to see that someday."

"Excuse me, I would like to borrow Austin for a minute. Other people would like to meet him." Gwen took Austin's hand and led him away.

"Thanks, you're a life saver."

"Don't thank me yet. Your smile and your handshake are about to get well worn out."

They stopped in front of a large man, tall and wide. He took Austin's hand and put it in a death grip. *Ow.*

"Austin, I'm Bruce. I'm so glad to meet you. I know your father has looked long and hard for you. It's great that he finally found you. You look great. Are your wounds healing?"

Pulling back his hand, Austin rubbed it, then flexed his fingers to make sure they still worked. "Yes, fine, thank you. It's nice to meet you too."

Twenty to thirty more people came to shake his now-sore hand. Austin smiled at each one, fielding questions from, "Why were you hiding out?" to gunshot wounds. A few wanted to see the scar, but he declined, not wanting to undo his tie that Gwen and Albert had helped him tie.

One woman had said that her husband wasn't going to come with her to church until she told him Albert's son would be there, then he hurried to get dressed.

A half-hour had passed when Albert announced, "Let's go home."

"Yes, please," Austin replied.

In the car, Gwen mentioned, "Carol asked to come over. I told her we were busy, so we need to go and do something."

"Great," Albert replied. "Let's head down to Key Largo and make a day of it. Call up Snook's and make reservations for tonight."

"I'm on it," Gwen replied.

On the way down, they stopped at a fast-food place to tide them over until dinner time. They stopped at a state park near Largo Sound. Taking some of the trails through the park, Austin kept envisioning a large alligator around the next corner waiting to gobble them up, but since no one else seemed concerned, he kept going. There were a few boardwalks over the vegetation where they could look out over the ocean.

"Of course, the best way to see Key Largo is by boat," Albert said. "Gwen and I took a glass-bottomed boat out to Molasses Reef. It was amazing. We'll have to do that again sometime."

"I would like that," Austin responded.

When they finished there, they headed over to the restaurant. They were given a table close to the shoreline. Several people from the condominiums across the cove were playing under a cabana. They jumped in the water or were pushed, on occasion. Austin watched them while he waited to order.

"How may I help you?" a smiling waiter came over to them.

"I'll take the big belly burger," Austin said.

"Oh, no, you don't." Gwen snarled. "We didn't come to one of Key Largo's best seafood restaurants to have you order a burger."

"Come back to me," Austin told the waiter.

Chapter Thirty-Six

Austin ended up ordering the fried seafood platter with crab, shrimp, and mahi-mahi. He loved it.

Darkness had fallen by the time the left the restaurant. "I've got to get you two home. You're starting work in the morning." Albert flashed them a big smile which Gwen returned.

That evening, Austin again looked up the trial of Mr. Russo. *They've set a date, one month away. I'll have to find a reason to get off work. I'm going to see her again!*

The next morning, Albert handed Austin a polo shirt with the car lot's name on it. "I have three more for you at work, but put this on for now."

Austin did. Soon, Gwen came down the stairs in the exact same shirt, except a lighter color. "Oh, I didn't know you had changed the shirts, Dad."

"You have to mix things up once in a while. Grab breakfast and then head down to the lot. I've already eaten, so I'll see you later." He picked up his car keys and left.

"I'll cook." Gwen volunteered. She cooked up four perfectly made sunny-side-up eggs with bacon, toast, and grits. "Here, I wanted you to know what you've been missing out on."

"Oh, good job on the eggs." He pointed. "What's the white stuff?"

"Grits. Dad loves them and puts butter and salt on his. I put honey on mine. He shudders every time I do it though, so don't let him see you."

Austin picked up a small amount on the tip of his spoon and tried it. "Pass the honey, please."

"Hi, Rich. This is Austin. He's our new…"

"Albert told me all about him. Get him started."

"Okay." She whispered to Austin, "That's Rich, the sales manager. He's in one of his bad moods. The good news is, they don't last long." Gwen showed Austin the table he would be sitting at. It had a computer, a file cabinet, and three chairs besides his. "The most important thing to remember is, never ask the customer if they want to buy a car."

"How do I know if they want to buy a car if I don't ask?"

"It's just a matter of taking them to the next step and overcoming objections along the way. When they come in, you show them all the cars they want to see. If they like one of them, then get them on a test drive. If they like the test drive, get them inside and start working the numbers. If they agree on numbers, then we check their credit if they are financing or send it to the finance manager if they have cash. That's it, it's that simple."

"People have enough money to pay cash for a car?"

"Yes, lots of people."

"Wow."

"Here, let me show you how to fill out the loan application." She pulled a piece of paper out of her pocket. "Here is the user name and password Dad set you up with. Go ahead and log in." For an hour she went over the process of paperwork. "If they're paying cash, you just need to fill in the highlighted sections." She watched him for another minute. "Great, it looks like you have that down. Let's go out on the lot and I'll teach you all about the features of each car."

"That sounds hard."

"Nah, you picked up the computer programs ten times faster than the other salesmen here. You pick up things really well. Hop in." As she drove around town, she turned on the active cruise control. "I have my foot off the brake, look what happens." The car slowed down and stopped when traffic backed up.

"What? You braked, didn't you?"

"No, the car did all that. You have the same feature in your car. You just need to turn it on." When traffic moved again, she took her hand off the wheel. "See, the car steers to keep you in the center of the lane. You want to turn that off on winding roads though or you'll be fighting the car to steer it."

She pulled into a parking space and had him drive back to the lot, making him use all the features she had just described. Then they walked down the row of used cars and she pointed out features of each one.

"Wow, there's a lot to learn," he replied.

"You don't need to worry too much about the used cars, those will come later, but the new ones you'll need to know all about. I have videos and instructions for you to go through to become certified in all the new cars, then you can start selling."

"Okay." She had him log in again. "There you go."

As he went through all the exercises, another salesman came up from behind him. A short blond-headed kid. "What are you doing?"

"I'm certifying."

"You don't need to worry about that. You won't be around long enough to finish."

"What?"

"Most guys wash out in the first three months."

"I don't think I'll be washing out. I don't have that option."

"You're that far in debt, huh? Trust me, this is a rough business, especially with old man Morgan constantly breathing down your neck, and that daughter of his, don't get me started on her. Besides, I've been here six months and I haven't bothered finishing up my certifications. Nobody cares."

Gwen came up to them, "Hi, Mike. I see you've already met my brother, Austin."

"Br...brother? I didn't know he was your brother."

"Yes, my long-lost brother. Oh, by the way, Dad says to do nothing else until you get your certifications done. He's tired of reminding you." She walked off.

"Now, what were you telling me about certifications and my sister?"

"Never mind." Mike went back to his desk and pulled up the certification tests.

Two hours later, Austin had finished his certifications. Mike still sat there working on his. He spied a customer on the lot and stood up.

"Oh, no, you don't," Gwen glared at him. "The customers are for the certified salespeople. Go ahead, Austin."

Chapter Thirty-Seven

Austin swallowed and then stood up. He trotted out onto the lot. "How can I help you today?" to the man and his wife and their three kids. The kids scattered to the wind and began to play in different cars. The wife also headed in the opposite direction from the man. Not knowing what else to do, Austin stuck with the man.

"I need a Forester with tan leather seats."

"Let's see," he and the man looked at all the Foresters. "I don't see anything on the lot, but my sister works here, too, and she says we can trade with other dealers. How about we get you one, it'll be here in a couple of days."

"That won't work. I need it today. I have to take it to work tomorrow."

"Okay, great. We'll find the one you want at another dealer and I'll go get it for you while you're doing the paperwork."

The man thought for a minute, then motioned to his wife and whistled for the kids. "Come on, we're going inside."

Gwen took over the credit report as Rich sent him down to do a dealer trade at a nearby car lot. He came back on the lot with just enough time for the lot attendants to wash the car and get it ready for the customer before they came out of finance.

Albert walked out of his office and looked at Rich. "First customer sold. I didn't even do that well."

"The kid's a natural. He knew what to say even though he's never had any experience in that sort of thing."

A month later, both men looked up at the sales board. "Gwen's leading, but Austin's giving her a run for her money," Rich said. "They've both left Mike and the rest of the pack in the dust."

Gwen walked into the room. "Oh, sorry, I didn't mean to disturb you."

"No problem. Do you need something?"

"I guess this is for both of you. Austin is going to sneak out of the house tomorrow. He thinks he's going alone, but I'm going with him. You're going to be without two of your salespeople for a few days."

"What? Where are you going?" Albert blurted out.

"His girlfriend is testifying in court in a few days and it's his only way to see her again. He thinks he's driving to Chicago, but I bought tickets. I've been following the trial and watching him. He'll leave tonight sometime. I thought he'd take me with him, but his bags are packed and he hasn't said anything to me. I guess he hasn't figured out how manipulative big sisters can be."

"That girl's trouble," Albert replied.

"Yes, she is."

"I'm guessing I can't say no to this?"

"Oh, you can say all you want, but it won't change anything."

Rich snickered under his breath.

"Can we do without your two best salespeople for a few days, Rich?"

"Mike's been wanting extra hours so he can try to catch up. We'll be fine."

Albert put his hand on Gwen's shoulder. "Go with him and keep him safe."

"I will, Dad."

She walked out. Albert turned to Rich. "That girlfriend of his is the one who got him shot. I don't want him anywhere near her."

"Did your parents approve of your wife? Did you listen to them?"

"No and no. It turns out, they were right about her. I should have listened. I guess love is blind after all. I hope this turns out well."

"Me too, I need them to sell more cars."

Austin opened his door and scanned the hallway. Seeing the coast was clear, he edged out of the door. Shoes in hand so he wouldn't make any noise, he lifted his suitcase and tiptoed down the stairs. He stepped into the kitchen only to stop dead in his tracks.

"Going somewhere?" Gwen sipped her coffee while sitting at the table.

"I was, um, just getting a snack."

"With a suitcase. Come on. Go put that in my car. I'm packed and ready."

"I need to do this alone." He folded his arms.

"And how are you going to get there? Did you know there are toll roads between here and there? Do you even know how to handle those?"

"Okay, I don't have everything planned out as well as I thought I did."

"I have airplane tickets." She held them up.

"Oh. I wasn't looking forward to a twenty-hour drive. You've got a deal. What are we going to tell Dad, though?"

"I've got that handled, too. Bring your suitcase and put it in my car. I'll drive us to the airport."

He did as she said. When they hit the road, he asked, "How did you know?"

"I have the internet, too. All I had to do is look at your search history and see when the trial was, then wait for you to make your move. I walked by your room yesterday and saw your suitcase on the bed, so I packed mine."

"You checked my search history?"

"That's what big sisters do. I think, anyway. I haven't been one that long."

He shook his head.

She parked the car and they went through security after checking their bags. The plane boarded soon after they arrived at the gate. Sitting by the window, he leaned over to Gwen. "If you would have told me a year ago that I would meet a wonderful girl, be living in Miami, that I have a father and sister, and would be flying on planes all across the country, I would have laughed in your face."

"Well, at least you landed well after your mother's death. You would have been surprised there, too."

"I knew she was very sick. I tried to get her to go to the hospital but she didn't want to spend the money. I didn't know we were behind on rent. Her death shook me to the core, but it wasn't that unexpected."

"I'm sorry for the childhood you had to live. Things are better now. Are you still sad about the death?"

"No, I'm more upset. It hurts to know she kidnapped me."

She leaned over and put her arm around him. "I'm so sad for you."

Nodding, he swallowed hard. Blinking a few times, he turned to look out the window.

When they landed, they picked up their bags then walked out to get a taxi. "I tried to rent a car, but you have to be twenty-five to do that in most places. They don't like renting cars to twenty-year-olds. We have a hotel near the courthouse so we can walk back and forth to it. They have kept the day she's going to testify a secret so none of grandfather's gang will know when she'll be there."

"Oh, all right."

That night when Austin came out of the bathroom his sister lay asleep in the bed. He slid into his own bed quietly so as not to disturb her. *At least she doesn't snore like Ricardo does.* He snuggled down and went to sleep.

Chapter Thirty-Eight

Austin and Gwen sat through the trial for three days listening to forensic testimony and blood splatter experts. The detectives also testified in the trial of Louie Russo. It was all setting the stage for the main event, which would be, of course, Sophia's testimony.

When the courtroom filled with U.S. Marshals, Austin knew she would be next. She gave a hesitant smile as she entered the courtroom. Gazing out on the jury and then on the crowd, she gasped when she saw Austin.

Was that a good gasp or a bad gasp? He wondered.

The prosecuting attorney jumped up as the marshals rushed Sophia back out of the room. He couldn't hear what the prosecutor said to them, but he could see she didn't like something about the situation.

The judge rapped his gavel down on the desk. "I'm going to have to the clear the courtroom. The jury will head back into the jury room and everyone in the audience will please make your way through the back door in single file."

"This isn't good," Gwen whispered to him. "I wonder what happened? She is cute, though. Now that I've seen her."

When Austin walked through the back door a large man took him aside. "Here he is. You will come with me." When Gwen followed, he said, "Who are you?"

"I'm his big sister. Dad sent me with him to protect him."

Before the large man could respond, three marshals soon surrounded them. "Arrest this man for witness intimidation."

"What!" Austin replied.

"Hold it right there." Goose joined the fray. "I think this kid has suffered enough. We'll leave him alone."

"But…" the one marshal said.

A supervisor stepped into the middle of the circle. "Goose, is this the guy who was shot?"

"It's him, Sir."

"Let's all back off here. Goose, escort him outside so we can get this trial back on track."

"Yes, Sir." When they were in front of the courthouse, Goose said, "You can't be here, kid."

"I see that. I just wanted to say hi."

"I know. We've tried to keep your identity from the Russo Gang. The less they know about you the better."

"How did you come to be here, Goose? I thought you were taken off the case."

"Sophia requested me. The other guy totally mishandled the situation. Now, go back to Florida. You're not safe being here."

"But…"

"Go on."

Austin hung his head and walked away. Gwen put her arm around him. "At least she looked excited to see you."

"Excited? She looked scared to death."

"No, silly. She wasn't scared for herself; she was scared for you. Now let's get out of here before the bad guys figure out who you are."

"You really think she was scared for me?"

"Of course, I do. I'm a girl. I know these things."

"But how will I ever find her again?"

"You won't. She'll have to find you. I wouldn't get my hopes up though. She might stay in witness protection for years and even when she does come out of it, she might avoid being seen with you so she doesn't endanger your life."

Austin quickly wiped a tear away. "You're saying, I should give up."

"Basically. Carol likes you. She's kinda cute."

"She's way too aggressive for me." He looked down at the ground. "I want to go back to Idaho for a week. I want to walk down familiar streets. I want to see Ricardo again. I want to center myself with the familiar. Then I'll go on with the rest of my life without Lisa."

"You mean, Sophia."

"I don't know Sophia. She looked exactly like Lisa, but before the shootout, life was so much simpler."

"Can I come with you?"

"Of course, on one condition."

She gave him a sideways glance. "What's that?"

"Don't fall for Ricardo."

She laughed. "I'll try not to. That's the best I can do. He is a hunk."

Austin sighed. "If that's the best you can do. I guess we can go during the last week of summer break. I mean, they were going to replace us at the car lot by then anyway."

"I think I could talk Dad into that. Meanwhile, I'll make reservations for our return flight home. I'm not feeling like we're wanted here."

He smiled. "Thanks for coming with me. It was wrong of me to try and leave you behind."

"Yes, it was. You'd have a twenty-hour drive ahead of you. I'm much better at this traveling thing than you are."

When they arrived back in Florida, Albert greeted them. "Welcome home. Tell me all about it."

Austin shrugged. "Not much to tell. We got kicked out of the courtroom."

"No," Gwen shook her head. "It was more like they kicked us out of Chicago."

"True, basically, the whole state of Illinois," Austin replied.

"Wow, what did you do?"

"Nothing." Austin sat down on the sofa. "We just sat in the courtroom. She came in and saw me. They hauled her back out and then cleared the courtroom. They were waiting for us when we walked out."

"They threatened to arrest Austin," Gwen added.

"For what?"

"Witness tampering. Goose saved the day. It's a good thing I didn't punch him in the nose like you told me to."

"Yes. Well, let's go out to dinner and you can fill me in on all the rest of the story. I'm glad you didn't get arrested, Austin. I would have had to come up there and straighten things out."

"I'm glad, too."

Chapter Thirty-Nine

The day Austin walked back onto the car lot; Rich handed him an envelope. "You forgot to pick this up before you left."

"What is it?"

"Your paycheck."

He sat down at his desk and opened it. *Five thousand?*

Gwen sat down across from him. "Can I see?" He handed her the check. "Not bad for your first month. We'll work on that for next month."

"Not bad? How much did you get?"

"A couple of thousand more than that."

"I thought I was working for room and board. I didn't even know I was getting paid."

She giggled. "You didn't know you were getting paid? Of course, you're getting paid. Well, not as much as me."

"I don't get it. Dad provides for my every want and need and then he pays me on top of it. What a raw deal for him."

"He loves you, silly. You sell more cars than everyone but me."

"I'm not used to this money thing."

"There's a customer on the lot, go get him."

Austin stuffed the check in his pocket and headed out.

Albert had been agreeable to them going back to Idaho, but in exchange, he wanted them working weekends while they went to school to make up for it. When midterms and finals came, he would let them have off to study.

He drove them to the airport and wished them luck.

On the other end, Ricardo picked them up in Spokane. "Little buddy, it's so great to see you. I didn't get to say goodbye to you when you left the last time." He hugged him. Turning to Gwen, he hugged her. "Little buddy two."

"So that's who I am now?"

"Yep. I've freed up my weekend for you guys. Where do you want to go first?"

"I want to visit Mom's grave."

"Sure, hop in."

They drove down the familiar road and stopped in the graveyard. Looking at the stone that Albert had purchased for her, Austin couldn't hold back the tears. "Can I have a moment alone?" he asked.

Gwen and Ricardo stepped back.

"I loved you. I trusted you. My whole life was a lie. You didn't let me get to know my father and my sister. You kept them from me. If you hadn't died, I still would not have met them. You were selfish by keeping me from them." He wiped some tears. "This is the last time I'll visit you. I'm sorry, but I feel so betrayed." Turning, he walked back to the others. "I'm ready to go."

"Where to now?"

"Let's go over to the hotel so we can dump off our stuff and change into our swimsuits, then I want to go out to Honeysuckle Beach."

"That sounds fun. Can I bring my sisters?"

"Absolutely."

With five of them in the car, the back seat was shoulder to shoulder. Like a good little brother, he had let Gwen sit up front. Ricardo's sisters were not small people though. Soon the group splashed in the waters of Hayden Lake.

"I learned to swim right here," he told Gwen. "We often came down here on hot summer days to cool off."

"This is awesome. The water is so blue, but it is a little chilly."

"It works better if you stay in it." He pushed her off the dock. As she fell, she grabbed his arm and they both ended up in the water.

After a few hours, Ricardo dropped them off back to the hotel to change. Later on, the three of them went out to dinner together.

"Well little buddies, what's the plan for tomorrow?"

"I thought we'd go to Triple Play Park. I've never been there."

Ricardo's smile disappeared. "I don't know why I didn't think of bringing you on one of our family outings there. We go several times a year."

"Because your family outings are for your family. Anyway, it doesn't matter. I get to go tomorrow."

"Okay, little buddy. See you then."

As soon as he left, Austin called a taxi.

"What are you doing? Gwen asked. "We could have had Ricardo drop us off."

"I don't want him knowing what I'm about to do. He'll think I'm silly."

"Oh."

When they arrived on Honeysuckle Avenue, Austin pointed things out for her. "Down there is the grocery store where Mom died. Down this street is where I used to live. The house with the large black truck in the driveway." They walked down a few feet. "Here is where I saw the goddess for the first time. She was sunning herself in the backyard."

"She didn't mind you looking at her?"

"Oh, I think she did because she got up and started to run for the house when she saw me, but then stopped and giggled at me when Goose came out and told me to get lost."

"Oh, dear."

"But then she waited for me the next day. She hid in that tree and started talking to me as I walked by. She must have been so lonely."

"She hid in a tree?"

"Yes, she didn't want Goose to see her talking to me."

"Had you known now what you didn't know then, would you still have tried to be friends with her?"

He thought for a minute. "I didn't much like getting shot, but I think I would have still gone for it. Knowing she likes me makes it all worthwhile. She was the first girl to pay much attention to me. The girls in high school just thought I was a kid who came from the poor side of town." Looking down the street to his old house, he added, "I had to come back to see if it all was real. My past life seems like a dream to me now. A very bad dream."

Chapter Forty

After a fun day of go-cart driving, swimming, and miniature golf, they headed for lunch. "I want to go back up to Spokane Mountain this afternoon," Gwen said. "We don't have mountains in Florida."

"Okay." Ricardo smiled. "And on your last day, we can go to the U of I to check out the college you almost went to and then on to WSU to check out the college I'm going to."

"That sounds fun," Austin replied. Gwen looked a lot less enthusiastic but didn't say anything.

At the top of Mount Spokane, they played with a frisbee Ricardo had brought with him. Gwen had to sit down a few times because the altitude made it hard for her to catch her breath. They also walked through Vista House and looked out at the countryside.

"This is beautiful," Gwen said. "I want to travel when I graduate from college. Will you come with me, Austin?"

"Yes. I've gone from never leaving my hometown to flying back and forth across the country. I'm ready for some international stuff."

When they arrived back in Hayden, Ricardo dropped them off at the hotel. He had plans for the evening.

At dinner in the hotel, Austin asked, "How's it going with not falling for Ricardo?"

Gwen smiled as she shook her head. "He didn't tell you? He's got a girlfriend. That junior he talked about, I guess she's a senior now. Anyway, that's the one. That's where he is tonight."

"I can't picture Ricardo dating just one girl. Wow, things have changed since I left. One more day, Sis."

She reached across the table and put her hand on his. "For years I dreamed about finding my little brother. I wondered what it would be like, our relationship, I mean. Not only have I found my little brother, but I've found a good friend, too."

He swallowed, "Thanks, Sis. You've been a great friend also. Oh, and also a protector, a rescuer, and someone to get into trouble with. That's very important in a boy's life."

She laughed and went back to eating.

The tour of the campuses had been fun for Austin, but a little sad, too. Instead of being only seven miles from his best buddy, he would be across the country. He wondered how long their relationship would last with being so distant. A few letters and phone calls, other than that they would be growing apart.

Austin sat back in his plane seat. He had given Gwen the window seat but regretted it. She had fallen asleep ten minutes into the flight and hadn't woken since.

College. The very thought of it sent shivers down his spine. *Am I ready?* He wanted to do well because his father was footing the bill for it and he didn't want him to be upset.

The seat belt sign came on accompanied by the sound. Gwen sat up. Looking out the window, she asked, "I see water. Where are we?"

"Almost there."

"Wow, I missed it."

Albert stood in the middle of baggage claim when they came out. He ran over and hugged them. "Boy, that house gets awfully lonely without you two there."

"Hi, Dad," Gwen said.

"Thanks for picking us up," Austin replied.

"You guys start school on Monday. Are you excited?"

Gwen nodded, but Austin sighed. "More scared than excited. But I was scared the first day of high school, too. I'll have Gwen there to help me out."

She put her arm around him. "You bet you will."

The next day Austin sat at his computer when Gwen walked by his room. "What are you doing, little brother?"

"I'm just seeing how the trial went. In Sophia's testimony, she says her father tried to go straight, but the grandfather didn't trust him because he knew too much. She overheard him order the hit on her father. That's when she fled out of the house and never returned."

"That's terrible, the old man killed his own son."

204

"They found him guilty of murder, racketeering, money laundering, and a whole bunch of charges. She wasn't the only person who testified against him."

"So, what happens now?"

"I guess she stays in hiding the rest of her life. I don't know."

"You need to move on, Austin."

He hung his head. "You might be right."

Austin sat at the food court waiting for Gwen to get there so they could have lunch together. Seeing some downtime, he broke out his books and began to study. Gwen had taken him all over campus and showed him where all his classes were and then all the major buildings. She didn't leave him alone until she knew he could get around. His first week of college convinced him he could handle it. It was just like high school, only with more homework.

A dark-haired girl stood in front of him. "Do you know where the library is?"

Another lost freshman. This was the third time that day he had been asked for directions. Without looking up, he pointed, "Down the steps to your right. Half a block down. You can't miss it."

To his surprise, the girl stayed there. He looked up. Something about her seemed familiar.

"Does it hurt still?" she asked.

"What? Does what hurt?"

"Your shoulder."

He stared at her a minute more. "Lisa?"

"I guess you can call me that. My real name is Sophia. I never told you it, but somehow you figured it out."

He stood up and threw his arms around her. "Is it really you?"

"Yes."

They sat down arm in arm. "I thought I'd never see you again. What if they catch you? Are you going to school here? How awful was that trial, huh?"

"Wait," she held up a hand. "One question at a time. Grandpa suffered a heart attack soon after they put him in prison. He didn't make it. The gang had no real leader and most of them also wound up in prison. I'm safe enough, I guess. I'm not going to school this semester, but I start here in the spring. I thought I was going to U of I, but Goose tracked you down here, so here is where I came. Goose used his marshal credentials to get your class schedule. I hope you don't mind. I sat outside your last class to surprise you, but you walked right by. I guess the hair color threw you. You were my only friend through an awful period in my life and even now. My whole life is upside down. I can't go back to Chicago. Too many memories."

"You really registered here because of me?"

"Austin, what are you doing with that girl?" Carol shrieked. "I thought we were together."

"Carol, we were never together."

"I wanted us to be together." She stomped her foot then stormed away.

"Who was that?" Sophia asked.

"She's a friend of my sister's. She's been chasing me ever since I came here."

A few minutes later Gwen came and sat down at the table. "Oh, wow, hi, Sophia. You changed your hair."

She smiled. "This is my natural color. They dyed my hair when I went into witness protection."

"Looks great. Austin, I asked Carol to have lunch with us. I hope you don't mind."

"You missed her. She stormed off right after she saw Sophia."

"Oh, that's not good. I'll have to patch her up again. I can do that later. What are your plans now that you're back together?"

Austin shrugged. Sophia answered. "Austin didn't even recognize me at first. I guess we start over. He knew me as Lisa, so now I have to introduce him to Sophia. I don't know if he'll even like Sophia, but I hope he will."

He squeezed her tight. "Of course, I will. I get a chance to meet the real you."

The End

See the sample chapter for

Bullets and Blondes **below**

Other Books by Clark Graham

Time Loop Series
A Loop in Time
A Hole in Time
A Rift in Time

Galactic War Series
End of the Innocent
The Last War
Invasion

Elvenshore Series
Dwarves of Elvenshore
The Lost Cities of Elvenshore
Elf's Bane
The Last of the Minotaur
Curse of the Druid King
War of the Druid King
Dwarves Druids and Dragons
Return of the Druid
The Last Druid

Wizard Series
Wizards and Heroes
Trouble With Dragons

Time God Series
Apprentice to the Time Gods
The Youngest Time Gods
Death of a Time God

Other Books
A Witch's Revenge
Bullets and Blondes

Children of the Gods
Emily and the Shadow King
International Mysteries
Millennium Man
Moon Over Mykonos
Murder Beneath the Palms
Nick Spool: Galactic Private Eye (Free)
State Secrets

Bullets and Blondes

Chapter 1

It doesn't mean anything. Barry Hibbard tried to reassure himself as he looked at all the pottery pieces spread across the floor. He had known better than to leave the vase on the pedestal after the last close call. Instead of putting it in a safer spot, he had become more particular as to who he allowed over. This guest, however, was uninvited.

He turned back towards her. She was beautiful, with penetrating blue eyes and smooth skin. Blond hair stuck out past the edges of the gray hoodie. Her features reminded him of a porcelain doll, but, unlike most porcelain dolls, this one had a shotgun.

When he heard the crash, he was almost asleep. It was something that took more and more effort after all the stresses he had endured during the past year. He had grabbed a baseball bat out of the hall closet and then tiptoed down the stairs. When he reached the bottom, he'd flipped on the light, revealing the intruder. She pointed the gun at him. Instinctively he dropped the bat and raised his hands over his head.

"Where's the Rex battery?" she demanded.

"The what?"

"Don't play stupid with me, buddy. I want the battery."

"I am stupid. I don't know what you are talking about."

Propping the shotgun on her hip, she creased her forehead, pulling a crumpled slip of paper out of her pocket. "This is 2471 Country Club Lane, right?"

He motioned with his head, leaving his hands in the air. "Next door."

She turned pale, making her rosy cheeks stand out even more. "Sorry, I'm so sorry."

He just shrugged.

"I'll pay for your pot. How much?" She pulled out her wallet.

He'd paid twenty thousand for it, but it was insured for three times more. Unfortunately, he couldn't replace it for that amount. "Ninety seven thousand, five hundred."

Her mouth gaped open. "For an urn?"

"It's a vase. Ming Dynasty, Wan li period, made in the late 1590s."

She covered her mouth with her hand. "Oh, my goodness." She slipped the wallet back in her pocket.

"Don't worry, it's insured."

"Sorry," she said, and then turned and crawled out the same window she had climbed in.

He put his hands back down to his side. *It does, too, matter*, he thought, wiping back a tear. He listed all the things that had left, died, or broken during the year. First the wife, then the dog, and now the vase.

He'd known the latch on the window was broken for the last month. It was on his list of things to get fixed. It was a long list that also included the alarm system. It hadn't been a huge priority for him, until today. There was one thing he was going to do first, though.

"It's two o'clock in the morning," Raymond protested as he answered the phone.

"It broke."

"What are you talking about, and why are you waking me?"

"The Ming. It broke."

"That's too bad," the sarcastic voice said. "Oh, that *is* too bad." The tone brightened and Barry knew Raymond was calculating the commission in his head.

"I want another one. It's three in the afternoon in Paris. You can call one of the art houses there and have one on the way before I get back up."

"You're going to bed?"

"Of course, it's two o'clock in the morning." Not wanting to hear Raymond's rude reply, Barry didn't wait for an answer.

He walked over to the vase, looked down at the pieces and thought about gluing it back together. It wouldn't be worth anything in that condition, but Barry couldn't take another loss in his life right now.

As he gazed at it, he realized there were just too many small pieces. It would be up to the maid to clean it up when she got in.

Not wanting a repeat of the break-in, Barry went out to the garage and brought in a hammer and nail. With the window secured, he went back to bed.

As he lay there staring at the ceiling, too upset to sleep, his mind was racing. Something had to change. It was one loss after another, and he couldn't take it anymore.

A year ago, he had the ideal life. A supermodel wife, a rare Tibetan Mastiff dog, and a beautiful Ming Dynasty vase. Now all three were gone. The first two had left the same day. The wife stormed out, claiming he loved his things more than he loved her. She left the door open and the dog ran into the street and was run over. He had paid six thousand for the dog and the wife had cost him much, much more in the divorce.

During therapy, his psychologist kept mentioning he shouldn't put a price tag on every aspect of his life, but he couldn't help it. Everything was assigned a value in his mind.

Luckily he had signed a prenuptial with the wife, so she didn't take him to the cleaners, but she still walked away with a cool million. Somewhere between five and six, as the sun was just coming up, he drifted off into a fitful sleep.